ALTERED DESTINY

AF520631

notionpress.com

ALTERED DESTINY

Suhas Inamdar

notionpress.com

Notion Press

5 Muthu Kalathy Street, Triplicane,

Chennai - 600 005

First Published by Notion Press 2014

Copyright © Suhas Inamdar 2014

All Rights Reserved.

ISBN: 978-93-84049-09-6

This book has been published in good faith that the work of the author is original. All efforts have been taken to make the material error-free. However, the author and the publisher disclaim the responsibility.

No part of this book may be used, reproduced in any manner whatsoever without written permission from the author, except in the case of brief quotations embodied in critical articles and reviews.

I dedicate this book to my parents, who have taught me how to think positively always

PREFACE

A lot has been written on the subject of the power of the sub-conscious mind in various languages by eminent authors. Even Hindu Mythology has a lot to say on this subject. Still, somehow, this subject has not gained popularity and acceptance among the masses as yet.

This book attempts to put forward the same concept in an interesting story format so as to generate enough interest on this subject, and with the fond hope that some people actually try it out as well.

It is rather strange that all of us have this tremendous power within us and still do not want to use it. It does not require any rigorous physical exercises, or a special kind of tasteless diet. It also does not require us to sit in a posture of penance for years together, as was narrated in ancient stories.

What it requires is only to 'think positively' and have 'faith and belief' in what we want to achieve. We need to 'Visualise' what we want with a 'sincere desire'. That's it. Nature's forces will then strive hard to create situations and circumstances which bring about the results as requested by us!

This is purely a work of fiction and readers may at times find resemblances with certain situations, places and characters, living or dead.

It is purely coincidental.

ACKNOWLEDGEMENTS

While publishing my second book, I look back over the road travelled and feel the need to acknowledge the active help and support of those around me, without which this book would not have been possible.

I thank my parents for their untiring efforts in shaping our future during our childhood.

I am grateful to my wife Sanjana for continuing to inspire me to write my second book. The same goes for my wonderful children, Sagar and Sampada.

I sincerely thank all my relatives, friends and well wishers who have personally communicated to me their feedback on my first book, 'Power Games of Life'. Their feedback has been very helpful in motivating me to write this book. It was very important for me to make sure that I avoided the same mistakes and also improved on my strengths. I hope to continue to receive their constructive feedback in the future as well.

I am thankful to Notion Press for publishing my second book.

And finally, I am thankful to the Almighty for…for everything.

Chapter 1

As Yashwant Rathore's car entered the Central Jail premises at sharp 9am, all the jail staff turned alert. Yashwant was very punctual and always reached office on time through all seasons of the year, including when it rained heavily. People would say that one could set the time on his watch by observing the Yashwant's arrival time at his office in the Central Jail.

Yashwant had been the jailor of Central Jail, Mumbai for the last eight years and during this period he had initiated and implemented several good measures inside the jail for the welfare and well-being of the prisoners. He believed that the prisoners too were human beings with emotions and feelings just like everyone else. He believed that many of the prisoners were basically good people without any criminal track record, but some circumstances in the past had forced them to become criminals, for which they were suffering now. Had they shown some restraint in those heated moments, they could have saved themselves and the people around them all the agony. Consequently, as one of the initiatives to reform the prisoners and to improve the quality of their remaining lives, he had arranged for special lectures on 'Anger Management' inside the jail premises. He believed that anger never helped anyone. When a person gets angry, his blood pressure rises, his heartbeat rises, he loses his balanced thought process and does many things impulsively, for which he would repent later on. The only situations where anger was justified and beneficial was when it was used to revolt against the unjust rule of the British in the pre-independence era or when a person failed to achieve something and then used his anger positively to derive positive feedback for his subsequent attempts to achieve his goal.

Yashwant walked to his office accepting salutations of all the staff that stood at attention as he passed them by. The staff had tremendous respect for him because of his benevolent personality. They were not afraid of him, as they knew that he was a value driven and principled person. This was in stark contrast with other senior officers in the department who derived their respect from their subordinates out of fear and force. All his actions were rational and not motivated by any personal or political gains. This was why many people wondered how a person like Yashwant had taken on this tough job of being a jailor, where he was required to monitor, manage and control all the prisoners. What surprised them further was that he had not changed his ideology or thought process even after spending 26 years of his service in various jails in different parts of India. Some of his staff also wondered whether he had been like this in his youth or whether, over the years his thought process had matured. Generally, the qualities of 'positive, balanced and rational thinking' are associated with older people while the qualities of 'fast, impulsive and rash thinking' are associated with young people.

It was not that such benevolent behaviour had ever stopped him from dealing sternly with the criminals whenever it was needed. His broad philosophy was that a good jailor is identified by his skill to segregate all the prisoners into two main categories – those who are in the jail because of habitual offences and secondly, those who are in jail because of a onetime offence committed in the heat of the moment. As a result, he acted differently while dealing with these two categories of prisoners. He was very strict with the habitual offenders while he tried his best to reform those prisoners who had committed one-off crimes. Which was probably why he could still continue in his job. Otherwise, if he had been soft on everyone, he would have either been bullied by the strong prisoners or transferred to other departments by the government authorities for inefficient handling of the prisoners.

He sat on his chair and opened the file in front of him. He had organised a system of getting a daily report which was required to be on his table every morning at 9am. The report contained all the important details like the number of prisoners lodged in the jail as on date, any new entrants/releases from the prison, the medical reports of those prisoners under medical care, stock of groceries and vegetables/fruits for the jail kitchen, any untoward incidents which had happened the previous night etc. A quick glance over the report file gave him the entire picture of the state and condition of the prison. Any efficient administrator, irrespective of the field he worked in, would require such reports for effective functioning of his department.

While he was sipping his first cup of hot coffee in the office, his desk phone rang. He looked curiously at the caller number and picked up the receiver. It was the Home Minister, Nandakumar Joshi.

After exchanging greetings and initial pleasantries, Nandakumar said, 'Yashwant, I want to ask you, how safe is your jail?'

Yashwant was confused. He did not quite understand the question.

Nandakumar continued, 'I am asking you this question because I have been asked to shift the dreaded terrorist, Dilawar Khan to your jail, as there are some specific intelligence inputs, warning that there could be internal and external attacks on Delhi Jail, where he is currently kept.'

Yashwant became slightly tense. He just said, 'Ok sir.'

Nandakumar said, 'I have not got the final orders as yet, but I thought of keeping you in the loop just to gauge your confidence level and preparedness to accommodate such a dangerous and high profile prisoner in your jail. Are you prepared?'

Yashwant said confidently, 'No problem sir, we shall manage it. We can provide adequate security to him and also the other prisoners from any kind of threat. I am prepared for this...'

Nandakumar thanked Yashwant and hung up.

Yashwant went into deep thought. So far, he had never held such a high profile terrorist in his jail. He needed to review the entire system and check every detail before he took the responsibility of assuring the safety of the prisoner. He remembered the brave and courageous act by the Delhi police who had gone to Kashmir based on a tipoff and nabbed him in a daring raid on the house, where he was discussing the plan of his next attack with his aides. The gun battle, which went on for almost seven hours, had finally ended with all his people dying in the attack while he was captured alive, though slightly injured. In fact, he too would have died, but the revolver which he used to kill himself had no bullets in it at that critical time when the police broke open the door and barged into the room in which he was hiding. The police were also quick enough to search his pockets within seconds of catching him, and took out the cyanide capsule which he had kept for using in such emergency situations. The team of police who led this operation was suitably rewarded later on, because the police department had been looking for him for several cases of terrorist acts, including three cases of serial bombings in the markets of different cities during the last 10 years and also for some extortion cases. After his arrest, the terrorists had suddenly gone into hibernation; they waited and watched to see what the next step of the government would be, as they wanted to plan their retaliatory actions depending on how the government dealt with him. It had been four months since he had been in police custody in Delhi and now they planned to shift him to Mumbai for security reasons.

Yashwant got up and went for his daily rounds inside various sections of the jail. However, his staff noticed that he was not in his usual mood today. Neither was he observing the minute things inside the jail as keenly as he always did, nor did he ask his habitual questions to his staff. He completed his round more as a duty than as a passion and came back to his office.

He called his assistant, Narayan to his cabin and asked him to bring the layout of the prison. He wanted to study the prison safety from a new angle in light of the perceived threat from inside/outside the jail to set free Dilawar Khan.

Yashwant was watching a TV serial at home with his family in the evening. He enjoyed spending time with his family and always emphasised to his staff that they should endeavour to spend quality time with their families. He believed that a person's job is only a means of his survival and gainful employment, but it should never take precedence over his personal life. One's personal life is meant for happier and caring moments which are to be shared with the near and dear ones in the family. These moments, he believed, were very precious and could not be exchanged with any other form of happiness in life. However, many people get so bogged down in their daily routine that they tend to either ignore or simply fail to appreciate these moments in life. Or sometimes, over the years, people simply do not cherish these moments.

Yashwant enjoyed his work but loved returning home to his family as well. He enjoyed the dynamic nature of his work, - dealing with the prisoners during the day, and also the peaceful moments spent with family after office hours. There are very few people in this world who actually find their office and home equally interesting. Many people hate going to office while some people loathe returning home. Incidentally, their happiness or lack of it at either the home or the office would automatically reflect in their performance in the other. For example, a person enjoying his work would generally have a peaceful family life and a person having a troubled family life would not perform well in his career.

His grandson, studying in 2nd grade, came running to him and showed him a 'star' which he had earned in his Maths homework that day. It was amazing to see that a simple star given by a teacher could have such a deep positive impact on the child and boost his confidence, morale and motivate him beyond limits. As usual, Yashwant looked at his grandson's notebook with full attention and praised him lavishly for earning a star.

He casually picked up the newspaper to read the political news. These days he read the political news for entertainment. The politicians were stooping lower and lower with each passing day to prove their point correct and the opponent's point wrong. The moral values in political circles across all the parties were falling steadily. Corruption was rising alarmingly. He had lost interest in these politicians a while back, when he dealt with some of the powerful political prisoners lodged in his jail. They had almost converted their cell in the jail into their guest house having all facilities and provisions. He observed their thinking and their behaviour at close quarters. He was amazed at their brazenness at times.

One advertisement on the fifth page caught his attention. It was about a seminar by a person named Yogeshwar on 'How to use the Powers of the Sub-Conscious Mind'. He read the details and was very impressed. According to Yogeshwar, if a person thinks positively continuously, then the sub-conscious mind of the person helps in bringing about positive changes in his life as well. It sounded very nice, but was it correct? How can things change if one thought positively always? Do our thoughts have any relevance to the outside world? If it be so, then is the world not governed by several millions of such thoughts of individuals, which makes it almost uncontrollable? Then how do we say that positive thoughts can change the events in a person's life? Does the same theory apply for negative thoughts as well? Which means, if everyone starts thinking negatively for a while, would the events turn increasingly disastrous, ending in a catastrophe? First of all, what controls the world? Is it the sum total of everyone's thoughts, or is there some other entirely different power, which we generally refer to as 'God', 'Luck', 'Fate' and 'Destiny' etc? What percentage of events is influenced by 'Collective Thoughts of Mankind' and what percentage is controlled by so-called 'Destiny'? That night he went to bed with these thoughts flooding in his mind. He was intrigued and curious to know more about this subject.

The next day, he went to the office as usual and started reviewing the drawings of various sections of the jail kept ready on his table by Narayan. He was carefully studying all the entry and the exit routes of the jail and also the separation of various zones within it. He wanted to be ready for the big event when Dilawar Khan would be shifted to his prison. He also reviewed the existing list of some 5,000 prisoners currently lodged in the prison. He went through the profile of some of the hardcore prisoners among them, to see whether any of them could try to either harm or help Dilawar Khan when he arrived there. He did not want to rule out any possibility, and considered every possible reaction of Dilawar Khan's entry into the prison, so as to be adequately prepared.

He went on rounds inside the prison to physically check the most sensitive part of the jail, called 'Anda Cell'.

The name of cell must have originated from its egg-shaped structure. The Anda Cell was monitored by CCTV round the clock. It had three layers of protection and one had to pass through 11 gates to reach the innermost barrack, which was considered the safest place, reserved for the most notorious criminals. History revealed that only the most dangerous criminals involved in high profile and sensitive cases were kept in this cell.

Yashwant was fairly satisfied with the arrangement there. Of course, when Dilawar Khan would be shifted there, the security would be more than doubled and all other gangsters currently lodged in the different cells around the Anda Cell, who could harm or help him, would be shifted to faraway cells so as to avoid any possible interaction between them that could lead to any eventuality.

Yashwant had just returned to his office when Nandakumar called him and confirmed that the final decision had been taken and the operation of shifting Dilawar Khan would be done quietly without any publicity to avoid any untoward adventures from unexpected quarters on the road while shifting him. Nandakumar also confirmed that this would be done sometime next week. He advised Yashwant to keep only the concerned senior officers informed of this decision with a warning not to divulge the information till it was done. Yashwant assured him that it would be done with all secrecy and hung up.

Finally the day came when Dilawar Khan was to be shifted to Anda Cell of Mumbai Central Jail. Yashwant had personally ensured that all potential risks were adequately mitigated. He got the entire kitchen facilities sanitised. All the walls of Anda Cell were tested through a metal detector and the gates were manned by additionally reinforced police personnel 24 hours before he was to be shifted. Metal detectors were placed on each gate and all the support staff was required to go through them, just like in airport security check-in. The aluminium plate, bowl and glass were replaced with plastic as he did not want to take chances with the unlikely scenario of Dilawar Khan trying to harm himself by converting the aluminium plate into a sharp-edged weapon by hitting it on the floor. The cooks were required to taste the food prepared for Dilawar Khan in front of the sub-inspector on duty before serving it to him. The shift timings of the security guards were made such that they had an overlap of one hour between any two shifts. Proper log books were introduced to record every minute detail inside the Anda Cell to help the investigations later, in case of any unforeseen incident.

At 3am on a Sunday, when the whole of Mumbai was sleeping blissfully and the roads were almost deserted, a cavalcade of nine vehicles entered the Central Jail carrying Dilawar Khan, who was brought to Mumbai in a chartered flight from New Delhi. A rarely used emergency route was used at Mumbai airport to take Dilawar Khan out, almost unnoticed by the sleepy airport staff, the crew members and the passengers arriving/departing at the airport.

Yashwant was prepared for this moment. This was one of the important moments in his service. He was entrusted with ensuring the safety of one of the most notorious criminal in the custody of the Indian government at that moment. And he was determined to do it perfectly.

Within a few minutes after Dilawar Khan was taken inside his cell and locked up, Yashwant walked up to the cell to have a glimpse of this dreaded terrorist. He wanted to see what a mass murderer looked like. He had seen many criminals in his career, but Dilawar Khan was a special case. He was by far the biggest criminal handled by Yashwant in his entire service. Yashwant asked the security guards to open the metal window of the cell so that he could see Dilawar Khan. The security guards moved the sliding window and through the strong steel bars, Yashwant could see Dilawar Khan sitting in the cell, resting against the wall, with one leg folded and one stretched out straight. At the sound of window opening, Dilawar Khan looked up at Yashwant and both of them looked at each other for few seconds. It was as if two unfriendly tigers were looking at each other in a jungle before attacking. The only difference was that here Dilawar Khan was caged and in captivity while Yashwant was in full control of the situation. However, by observing Dilawar Khan's cold look, Yashwant could make out that he was a ruthless, emotionless and dangerous criminal who could do anything...just anything.

It was difficult to figure out what was going on in Dilawar Khan's mind at that time.

Chapter 2

Over the weekend, one of Yashwant's old friends, Harish had come to meet him. Harish had been two years senior to Yashwant in college and was an all-rounder. He was a multi-talented personality who was equally good at studies, sports, elocution, drama etc. Which was why everyone in college, including Yashwant, had looked up to Harish. Harish went on to become an engineer and went to the US for further studies. After spending a few years there, he returned due to personal reasons and started a small consultancy business on improving manufacturing processes in continuous process industries. He had settled in New Delhi and travelled for business all over India. Whenever he was in Mumbai, he made it a point to meet Yashwant at his residence for lunch or a dinner.

After dinner that day, they were discussing general topics, when Yashwant referred to the advertisement he had seen in the newspaper about the seminar on using the powers of the sub-conscious mind. Immediately, Harish said, 'Yes, it is a very effective seminar. I have attended it last year and it works.'

Yashwant was surprised. Till then, he had believed that the seminar was someone's gimmick to make quick money by deceiving gullible people. But here was his friend who was saying that it was indeed effective.

Yashwant said, 'Come on Harish, do you mean to say that with just positive thinking, my sub-conscious mind can change the events around me?'

Harish replied patiently, 'Look Yashwant, I have attended this seminar and also an extended programme for 15 days, where they show you how to practice using your sub-conscious mind for positive thinking. Towards the end of program itself you will start seeing the results.

I am benefiting immensely from this programme. Of course, there is one note of caution though. Mere positive thinking is not enough; you need to put sincere efforts into your actions as well. And you need is to have complete faith in yourself and your actions. You will surely see results!'

Yashwant asked, 'Do you mean to say, if a student starts thinking positively about passing the exams with a distinction, he will really pass the exams with a distinction?'

Harish said, 'Of course, yes. However, he also needs to to study hard for this and mainly, believe that he will pass with distinction. And surely, he will...'

Yashwant was still not convinced. He felt that if a student studied hard, he would pass the exam by his efforts and not by positive thinking.

As if reading Yashwant's thoughts, Harish added, 'See, sincere efforts and a belief in yourself is a must. However, with positive thinking, you swing the balance in your favour. There is a thin line between 'something happened' and 'something almost happened'... Positive thinking has the power to remove the 'almost' word in between.'

That night Yashwant slept thinking about the power of the sub-conscious mind and positive thinking. He wondered whether people could make things happen around them just by positive thinking alone. There was a kind of mystery associated with this concept, since unknown powers were at play. He wanted to further explore these powers...

The next day, when Yashwant reached office, the Father from the local church was sitting there waiting for him. He remembered that it was that day of the month, when the jail used the services of the local church to counsel the prisoners. This was one of the initiatives implemented by Yashwant to reform the prisoners. The priest would meet some of the prisoners alone for 15 minutes and try to understand the reasons why they were there, and also instil some moral values in them. Analysis showed that the exercise was having a good effect, as the counselled prisoners had displayed better behaviour subsequently.

Yashwant went on his usual rounds and passed by the Anda Cell. He checked the log record on Dilawar Khan and observed that he had not created any trouble in the jail as yet. He asked the CCTV monitoring team whether they had noticed any difference in his behaviour or any suspicious movements in the past few days since he was brought here. They said that it was all routine behaviour. Dilawar Khan used to sit quietly in the cell most of the time. Sometimes he would pace the small cell like a tiger does inside the cage in a zoo. It was difficult to gauge, from his facial expressions or body language, whether he was planning something or repenting for his past sins. He always appeared cool from the outside; but observers knew that his mind was actually working at great speed.

Yashwant asked the constable to open the window of the cell. The constable promptly opened the steel sheet window pane. Now Yashwant could look inside the window through heavy steel bars. He did not spot Dilawar Khan from where he stood. So, he went a step closer to the window and suddenly Dilawar Khan stood up behind the window. He was smiling, exposing his yellowish teeth. Yashwant was startled for a moment.

Dilawar Khan said, 'What happened, Mr. Yashwant? Are you afraid of me?'

Yashwant kept looking at Dilawar Khan. He did not want to respond to him.

Dilawar Khan said, 'Mr. Yashwant, I have been lodged in several jails in my life. No jail could keep me for more than few weeks. See how I escape from your jail also.'

Yashwant was tempted to answer him, but kept his cool.

Dilawar Khan continued, 'You think that you are a great person, huh? All your security will be rendered useless the day I decide to escape from this place. Mind it!'

Yashwant could not restrain himself any longer. He said, 'You are so confident about your capabilities, Dilawar Khan? This is not any other jail. This is MY jail. And so long as I am the jailor, you cannot move out unless we release you.'

Dilawar Khan just smiled and said, 'Continue to live in your dream jailor, and save your energy to search for me on the day I vanish from here…'

Yashwant asked the constable to close the window and walked back to his cabin. He was in deep thought about the threats issued by Dilawar Khan. He was not sure how serious Dilawar Khan was and how seriously he should take his claims.

One thing was sure… the days ahead were going to be exciting.

Yashwant had enrolled himself for the five-day seminar on 'How to use the Power of the Sub-Conscious Mind and make Positive Changes in Life' after much contemplation. He was interested in knowing and learning about how positive thinking affected surrounding events. While sanctioning his leave, Nandakumar had taunted him, asking whether he wanted to reform the prisoners by using the new technique of positive thinking.

The five-day seminar was very enlightening for Yashwant. In the opening session of the programme, Yogeshwar had explained the three most important points about the programme. The first point was that all of us have a conscious mind and a sub-conscious mind. The second point was that the power of the sub-conscious mind was enormous, as high as 30,000 times the power of the conscious mind. The third point was that while the conscious mind was totally in our control, the sub-conscious mind was not in our control.

During the next five days Yogeshwar taught them the principles of the sub-conscious mind. Through this period Yashwant learnt a lot more about the concept of using the sub-conscious mind. He learnt that we can utilise the powers of the sub-conscious mind by constantly thinking something in our conscious state with complete belief that it will happen in reality. These thoughts from our conscious mind get transferred to the sub-conscious mind while we are asleep and the sub-conscious mind starts actively working on converting those thoughts into reality. And there comes the significance of positive thinking. If we continuously think positively while we are awake, the message gets relayed to the sub-conscious mind and it ensures that positive things happen to us. There is no other method to control the sub-conscious mind.

The sub-conscious mind derived its power from Nature's forces. All sub-conscious minds are connected to Nature's forces, just like all the landline telephones are connected to a telephone exchange. However, most people do not know how to use the power which is available within them. They can do wonders if they start using the power of the sub-conscious mind. There are several instances in history where incurable diseases were cured by the power of the sub-conscious mind; Fortunes were changed by proper usage of the sub-conscious mind and the impossible made possible.

There was also a procedure prescribed to practice this. The person is required to first relax, close his eyes, and breathe normally till the breathing becomes uniform and slow. Then he has to start saying the required objective in a positive affirmation, believing it and visualising it. For example, a person wants to buy a house, but he has no money to purchase it. In this case, he needs to sit in a relaxed position, close his eyes and start saying to himself, *'I have purchased a house'*, *'This beautiful house is mine'* etc. These thoughts will leave an imprint for the sub-conscious mind to work on. And then it begins acting. The sub-conscious mind has no reasoning powers. It cannot decide whether what you asked for is good or bad for you. Its task is only to effectively convert your thoughts into reality. Therefore, the thoughts need to be filtered so that the sub-conscious mind does not get triggered for some unintended and wrong purposes. That is why it is said that often, when people do not want something to happen, it happens. That is because, the sub-conscious mind looks at the thoughts which are negative and it blindly executes them. For example, it is recommended for a student to think 'I will pass' rather than 'I should not fail'. Because in the latter case, the scenario of failure appears in his thoughts, though it is to be avoided, and it prepares the ground for that.

Therefore, the Upanishads say, 'Watch out your thoughts, they define your destiny.' The logic was that repeated thoughts convert into actions; repeated actions convert into habits; repeated habits convert into our character; and our character defines our destiny.

Yashwant was now so interested in the subject that he immediately enrolled for a 15-day programme for detailed and extensive learning about the power of positive thinking. During this programme, all the concepts were explained in further details with some real-life case studies of its application as well. The case studies were mind boggling and further proved the theory.

One of the case studies was about an author who 'believed' that his book had become an international bestseller. He 'Visualised' *seeing the book on the bookshelves of reputed bookstores*. He started 'feeling' that *he was being invited to give a lecture on the inspirational contents of his book*. Subsequently, in due course, the book actually became a bestseller and the author earned a name for himself apart from the millions he earned from the royalties.

Another case study was about a body builder who 'Visualised' that *he becomes a successful movie actor*. He practiced this theory for a few days with complete belief and confidence that it would work. He also enrolled himself in a reputed acting academy. A plus point for him was that his body was in perfect shape. He started approaching movie producers and bagged a few good, small roles in the beginning. His acting was appreciated by the audience which fetched him bigger and more important roles, and he went on to become a superstar in a few years time. After enjoying a good stint in films, he developed an interest in politics and started 'thinking' of *becoming a Parliamentarian*. Again, after practicing this theory for a few weeks, he publicly expressed his opinion and his willingness to join a particular political party. The party was overwhelmed to get such a proposition from a popular face and welcomed him with open arms into their fold. He won the ensuing elections with a good margin. Subsequently, his life totally changed - from being a body builder to a cinema actor to a politician.

There was one more case study where a girl was suffering from cancer and her father tried every treatment available to cure her. However, nothing seemed to work. In desperation, he often used to say, '*I would give away my right hand*' if my daughter is cured of cancer. One day, in a gruesome accident, he lost his right hand, and instantly, his daughter was cured from the incurable disease. The doctors were unable to explain this phenomenon scientifically. In this case, his sub-conscious mind had 'conditionally associated' these two events of *giving away his right hand* and his *daughter's cancer* together and therefore, when one of them happened, the forces of nature acted strongly to bring about the other event.

After the programme, Yashwant started believing that he too could make changes happen in his surroundings. The concept was very simple. Our conscious mind is what we normally use while we are awake. It is fully in our control but has limited powers. Our sub-conscious mind gets active when we are asleep. It is not in our control but has infinite powers.

Now Yashwant wanted to apply these principles in his real life and experience the magical powers of the sub-conscious mind. He had by now developed total faith in this concept and had no doubts whatsoever about it. Moreover, this theory worked only on the premise that the person believed in this theory and also 'thought' about the desired outcome passionately and with full belief. Only then would it happen, otherwise not.

Yashwant was eager to start applying this mysterious theory into practice in his daily life and see it working. And if it really worked, then it would be amazing...he would be in partial control of his destiny. It was like going to a restaurant and ordering something from the menu card. Similarly, any of us can get up one fine morning and 'Think' in the prescribed way about a 'desired outcome' which we want. And the sub-conscious mind, like an obedient genie, would get it done for us. The powers of the sub-conscious mind are no lesser than those of a genie!

Chapter 3

Yashwant entered his office with a spring in his step. He was very enthusiastic about the new theory of science he had learned. He was eager to start applying it. He also recalled that in the programme it had been mentioned that when a person gained proficiency in using this power of the sub-conscious mind, then he automatically develops an ability to even read other people's minds, know the contents of an envelope without opening it or even experience travelling to distant places while physically being available at one place. That was a highly elevated status which required far more practice and he was certainly not qualified for that right now. But he had a sincere desire to reach that level one day.

He saw the daily log sheet and observed the number of sick prisoners currently undergoing treatment in the jail's hospital. As a first wish, he thought he should use his powers to cure the prisoners from their illness. He noted that there were 31 prisoners in the prison hospital suffering from various types of illnesses. He decided that as his first experiment he would 'Request' the sub-conscious mind to bring down the number to below 20. He wanted to test whether his sub-conscious mind had the power to cure other people. Theoretically, it could do anything. So, why not try this first?

That evening, he went home and sat in his study room. He had a small study room in his house as reading was his passion. His wife, Yogita and other family members respected his hobby and did not disturb him when he was in his study room, except when it was mealtime or he had been locked away in the room for too long. Excitedly, he decided to try out the theory. He sat in a relaxed posture in his armchair and closed his eyes. He stayed motionless in absolute tranquillity for about seven to eight minutes till his body stabilized and his breathing slowed down. Then he started slowly uttering the words, '*The number of patients in the prison hospital has reduced. The prisoners are getting cured of their health issues. The patients are being discharged after they become healthy and fit. The number of patients in the hospital is now below 20...*' He repeated these sentences in a low voice, as if speaking to himself, for around 15 minutes and then stayed silent for another five minutes. Then he emerged from the room and watched television with his family.

The next morning, he went to his office as usual, but with an altered confidence. He was supposed to have altered the destiny of some prisoners for that day. He had 'Actioned' his sub-conscious mind to heal some of the prisoners of their illness. He was sure of seeing positive results from his maiden experiment with this theory. One more reason for his confidence was that, by default, there was no room for any doubt in this phenomenon. One had to believe that it really happens. Otherwise, you are sending a confused signal to the sub-conscious mind and it will not act in the desired fashion. If we sit in a cab and ask him to go in three different directions, the driver will probably sit still. For the cab to move, the direction has to be clear. Similarly, the 'Thoughts' are required to be clear with full belief, with no 'ifs' and 'buts'.

Yashwant opened the log sheet and reached the hospital report page. His heart was thumping as he read the column mentioning the number of patients in the hospital. And the number of patients in hospital as of that day was...19. That meant that the previous day, during the night shift, the duty doctor had checked and discharged 12 patients. Yashwant was thrilled and happy. This was his first successful test of the theory of the sub-conscious mind.

It could have been a sheer coincidence; maybe these 12 patients were already getting ready to be discharged on that day. However, there was also a possibility that his 'sub-conscious mind' had actually worked as per his programmed thoughts. Anyway, he felt pleased with himself that he had indirectly helped those 12 patients to be cured faster than what they would have been otherwise. He also wondered for a second, whether he was interfering with God's scheme of things? However, the next moment, he felt somewhat relieved that he had used the power of his sub-conscious mind for a good cause - helping others - and not for any personal gains or malicious motives.

Thereafter, he started using the theory of the sub-conscious mind regularly for small things around him. For example, he had a habit of reading the headlines of the newspaper every day early in the morning. However, he had observed that of late, the newspaper was being delivered to his house at different times. He sensed an excellent opportunity to test his powers. He 'Visualised' that *the newspaper boy came at sharp 6.15am every day.* And to his surprise, within a week, he started getting the newspaper at 6.15am. Out of sheer curiosity, one day he casually asked the newspaper boy how he had become so prompt in delivering the newspaper over the last few days. The boy replied, 'What to do sir; my alarm clock was not working the last few days. Last week I purchased a new one and now I am able to get up every day at the right time.' Yashwant was unsure about whether his 'sub-conscious mind' had given the newspaper boy an inspiration to buy a new alarm clock or whether these two incidents had no connection at all. But the fact was that the desired result was obtained. And that is what mattered in the end.

Over the next few weeks, he used this theory on several other areas touching his daily life and surprisingly, it worked every time. Either there was a coincidence happening every time or the theory was working perfectly well. However, he slowly gained confidence that it was surely the theory of the sub-conscious mind working, and not just a coincidence, since coincidences also had a limit.

Yashwant had become friendly with many participants of his batch at Yogeshwar's programme and would meet them regularly, even after the programme was long over. They would share their experiences on using their powers of the sub-conscious mind. It was amazing and thrilling to hear their stories on their experiences about the results of positive thinking.

One of the participants said that he 'Visualised' that *he was eating sweets.* He visualised this thought for just three days and on the fourth day, his neighbour came to their house with a packet of sweets saying that his son had passed the exams with very good marks. Another participant mentioned that he started visualising that *he was in possession of rupees one thousand.* And after six days, while he was shopping in a mall, he won Rs.1,000 in a Raffle Draw.

These theories were inspiring everyone among this newly formed friends circle and they were trying it out as per their fancies and small dreams. And in all these cases, their desires were coming true, within a short span of just a few days. They were all very excited with these positive results and often wondered as to why everyone did not use this technique to realize one's dreams, small and big. They asked Yogeshwar this question. He gave a very simple reply: 'Almost everyone in this world knows that getting up early in the morning and going for a brisk walk is extremely good for health. In spite of knowing this how many people actually do this? Every student knows that by studying hard for the exams, he can obtain good marks. Yet, how many actually study hard during the year? Every smoker knows that smoking is injurious to health and may lead to cancer. Yet, how many smokers are able to get rid of their habit of smoking? Very few people can do this.' Similarly, today there are many books published on this subject of the power of the sub-conscious mind; there are several websites giving exhaustive details about the enormous power that can be derived by using this technique and yet many people do not know about it. Moreover, out of the people who know this technique, the majority does not believe in it and hence they do not try. This is really unfortunate. It is almost as if you have a lot of wealth with you, yet do not know how to use it.'

Subsequently Yashwant thought of going one step further - to use this technique on someone other than himself. He thought that it was probably easier to 'visualise' something for oneself and make it happen. However, if this theory can make a difference to others, then it would be considered as a really very effective theory. So, he started thinking about where he could test this now. And yes…he remembered that his maid, Sakhubai was an unhappy lady. She had worked with them for the past four years and was always complaining about something or the other. During their interaction with her over time, they had got to know the reasons for her unhappiness. Apparently, she had a desire to own a small house, but her financial condition was not strong enough to realise her dream. Moreover, her husband was addicted to drinking and used to abuse her every evening, under the influence of alcohol. There was no way she could have raised money to buy a small house, with only the support of her single income earned by working in different households. As a result, she was always unhappy. Yashwant said to himself, *I want to see her happy*. Let us see whether this theory works now. It was a very difficult challenge for this theory, because all the odds were stacked heavily against it.

Accordingly, Yashwant started visualising that *Sakhubai was enthusiastically working in his house and was smiling while talking to Yogita.* He visualised this scene with full belief, day after day. After about almost three months of this visualisation, one day, Yashwant noticed a difference in her behaviour. She was looking happy while working in the house and seemed to enjoy the work. Whenever Yogita asked her something, she replied with a smile on her face. Yashwant was now really excited to see that the theory seemed to work. He was curious to know how this had happened. The destination was apparently reached, now he wanted to know the route chosen.

One day, while having his morning tea along with Yogita on the lawns of his house, he asked Sakhubai, 'What happened Sakhubai, you seem to be very happy these days?' He was shocked to hear her reply. She said, 'Sir, I do not know which God has blessed me with his favours. My life is changing slowly. Around one month ago, my husband had an unbearable stomach pain. We were worried and went to see a doctor. The doctor examined him thoroughly and said that his liver was badly affected due to excessive drinking over the years. He also warned him that if he did not stop drinking liquor, then he would die soon. These words of the doctor worried my husband to such an extent that he stopped drinking altogether. Now it has been a week since he has touched liquor. He is slowly getting used to living without liquor.'

Yashwant and Yogita congratulated Sakhubai on this good news.

Sakhubai continued, 'One more thing, sir. I've been dreaming of owning a small house for my family for several years. But due to our weak financial condition we could not afford to buy one. Last week, I got a letter from my village mentioning that one of my maternal aunts had died due to old age. It seems my parents had sent me to her house when I was just three years old and I was raised by her in their house in my early childhood, which I only faintly remember now. Apparently she was very fond of me and liked me very much. She had no children of her own. Therefore, in her will, she has gifted me a small flat which she owned in the suburbs of Mumbai. I am so happy…my biggest dream in life has come true…'

Sakhubai continued talking but Yashwant was not listening to her anymore. He was overtaken by a strange feeling which was exciting, thrilling, mysterious and more. He had actually changed Sakhubai's life in just three months, without her knowledge, for the better. Was he God? Only God has such powers. However, here he had actually 'Visualised' certain things and they had happened. It was not a coincidence anymore. There had to be a science to this strange phenomenon.

Now he started getting worried. There were ample indications that this theory was working. And it worked perfectly. But then, how long would it work? Was the sub-conscious mind obliged to 'make things happen' for a limited number of times only? If that were so, then he would be wasting his newfound powers on trivial issues. Also, were there any specific guidelines for using it? As per Yogeshwar, these powers were most effective when used for the overall good of mankind, prosperity and growth of the society, etc. The powers were also useful for one as long as they did not result in harming someone. While it looked very exciting, he was slightly scared too - having such enormous power at his disposal that he could make changes in the lives of people around him without his physical interference. So long as a person doesn't have power it is alright, but once he attains such powers, he gets confused and worried about its proper usage and the possible backlash of improper usage.

One day, Yashwant suddenly remembered what Nandakumar had told him, while sanctioning his leave for attending Yogeshwar's programme. Nandakumar had half-mockingly asked whether he wanted to reform the prisoners by using this technique. He started seriously thinking about it now. There was no harm in using these powers for improving the life of prisoners, if it worked for their good, he thought. After all they are human beings and have the full right to live in society like normal people. With these thoughts, he checked the record of all the prisoners and selected the names of those prisoners who were scheduled to be released from the prison sometime next month. Then he filtered the list by selecting the most qualified and open minded among them. He compiled a batch of 10 such prisoners for this exercise and started teaching them the theory of bringing about positive changes in one's life by using the powers of the sub-conscious mind. He told them that each one of them had enormous power within him which could be used to change their lives. He advised them to start 'Visualising' the kind of life they wanted to live after they were released from prison. One of them said that he wanted to open a mechanical workshop, one of them wanted to drive an auto rickshaw. One of them had tailoring skills and wanted to open a tailoring shop. Yashwant asked each of them to evaluate their respective skills and then think about what they wanted to do. He taught them the technique of 'Awakening' the sub-conscious mind for helping them in attaining their mission in life.

Now only time would tell how accurately they were going to implement the theory and also whether they would gain any benefit from it.

Chapter 4

Yashwant was sitting in his office when Nandakumar called to enquire about Dilawar Khan. It was a routine call to ensure that there was no laxity regarding Dilawar Khan's security arrangements while in custody. After the call was over, Yashwant went on rounds. He went near the Anda Cell and asked the constable to open the window. Yashwant saw Dilawar Khan sitting inside the cell with no expression on his face. He did not look at Yashwant. Somehow, Yashwant wanted to speak to him and try to understand him. All the details about Dilawar Khan's crimes, as revealed by him during his interrogation, were already recorded in the Delhi jail, where he had been lodged for almost four months before he was shifted to Mumbai. Thus, there was no necessity for recording any more statements here. Yashwant went inside the gate which led him to Dilawar Khan's cell. The Anda Cell was constructed in such a way that there was a small area outside the cell from where one could talk with the prisoner inside. It was immediately outside the cell, separated from the cell by a fencing of heavy steel rods spaced four inches away from each other. There was a chair kept there for the police to have prolonged discussions with the prisoners during investigations without endangering their safety. Yashwant sat on the chair.

He asked Dilawar Khan, 'Dilawar, how are you? Are you facing any problems here?'

Without looking up, Dilawar Khan asked, 'How does it matter you Mr. Yashwant?'

Yashwant said in a pacifying tone, 'See, I am the jailor here and the well-being of all the prisoners is one of my prime responsibilities.'

Dilawar Khan did not react. Probably he was wondering why Yashwant had come to meet him today.

Yashwant said, 'Look Dilawar, the outside world is very beautiful. You can always forget your past and start a new life. If you live a life of dignity and honesty, you would enjoy your life much more. You need not be confined to a closed, small cell like this. This is not life…'

Dilawar appeared thoughtful. He asked, 'Which side did the sun rise today Mr. Yashwant? A jailor is preaching morality to Dilawar Khan?'

Yashwant replied, 'Dilawar, I can help you in reducing your jail term if you are ready to confess all your crimes and give us the names and addresses of all your gang members.'

Dilawar Khan suddenly rose to his feet and shouted, 'Get lost! Don't try to show sympathy for my current status. Do you think you will be able to retain me in here forever? It is just your imagination. I shall be gone very soon. And keep this moral lecture to yourself, Mr. Yashwant. Don't try to preach to me.'

Yashwant was stunned at this unexpected outburst from Dilawar Khan. He left the place and returned to his office. However, he kept thinking about Dilawar Khan and his behaviour. It was Yashwant's nature to try and reform every prisoner. And he had been doing this successfully all along. Several ex-prisoners were leading honest and sincere lives thanks to the values he had imparted to them. But Dilawar Khan was different. He was a hardcore criminal. He had committed several dreadful crimes in the past. He was associated with international gangs involved in terror attacks. It was difficult to change him. Something different was required to change Dilawar Khan.

And suddenly Yashwant remembered his newly acquired power of the sub-conscious mind. He thought for a while on whether it worked on hardcore people like Dilawar Khan. According to the theory, it should work.

But it looked difficult on the face of it. After some thinking, Yashwant thought, why not try using it and see? If it worked, fine. And if it did not work, then no problem! At least he would have the satisfaction of trying to use the theory on an extremely difficult case like Dilawar Khan.

That evening, Yashwant went into his study room as if he was on an important mission and sat in a relaxed position. After his body calmed down and his breath normalised, he closed his eyes and started saying, '*Dilawar Khan has reformed... He is a good person now... He is out of the jail now... The lives of many people have been saved because Dilawar Khan is reformed...*' He uttered these sentences in different combinations for almost 15 minutes with utter faith and belief, which was essential for this theory to work.

He had challenged the theory of the sub-conscious mind with the toughest task till date. No one knew whether this theory had been tried on such an improbable task earlier. According to the theory, this should be possible, because ultimately, the sub-conscious mind draws its Infinite powers from Nature to realise what is asked for with absolute sincerity and complete faith.

If the theory worked, it would be the biggest achievement of Yashwant's life. He would have not only reformed a hardcore terrorist but also saved the lives of many people, who Dilawar Khan would have killed if he were to get out of jail anytime. The thought was fascinating and exciting.

He did this repeatedly for almost one month, 'Visualising' that *Dilawar Khan's personality had transformed and he was now ready to mend his ways*. Then one day, he went to Dilawar Khan's cell and asked the constable to open the window.

As the constable opened the window, Yashwant peeped inside and found Dilawar Khan sitting inside the cell, resting against the wall. Sensing that the window was opened, he looked up and their eyes met briefly. For the first time, Yashwant noticed that Dilawar Khan did not look at him with hostility. He appeared cool. Yashwant did not understand at that point of time, whether 'The Power' had worked or whether Dilawar Khan was simply feeling low that day. He desisted from speaking to Dilawar and asked the constable to shut the window. He returned to his office.

After an additional three weeks of making his sub-conscious mind work on this assignment, he went to Dilawar Khan's cell again and sat in the well-protected area meant for discussions.

Dilawar Khan was lying down in his cell when Yashwant entered the discussion area. Seeing Yashwant enter the discussion area, Dilawar Khan got up and sat on the floor. He did not know why Yashwant had come there. Yashwant looked at Dilawar Khan and asked, 'How are you feeling today, Dilawar?'

Dilawar Khan looked at Yashwant and said, 'Fine, Mr. Yashwant. You came to ask me this question after a long time?'

Yashwant disregarded his question and continued, 'Are you comfortable here?'

'Yes, perfect. I am fine. I don't have any issues whatsoever.'

Yashwant thought for a moment about reminding Dilawar Khan about his challenge of escaping from the prison, but desisted as it would have changed the discussion into a conflict-like situation. He said, 'Dilawar, why do you do all these wrong things? What pleasure do you get by killing so many people?'

Dilawar Khan did not respond. He quietly stared at the floor.

Yashwant continued, 'Dilawar, every human being has a right to live in peace and happiness. And you have no right to snatch it away from them for your narrow-minded ambitions and mean goals. Do you know how many lives suffer when you carry out a bomb blast? Particularly when the breadwinner of the family dies in the incident, the whole family suffers. By the way, have you ever experienced pain in your life?'

For the first time, Dilawar Khan appeared serious in attempting to respond to Yashwant. He said, 'Mr. Yashwant, I have suffered so much pain in my childhood. We had no money. My father slogged throughout the day, working as a daily wage labourer, to earn money but it was barely sufficient for feeding the eight members of our family. And on the days he could not earn money, we all starved. I have undergone the pain of starving. Have you ever starved, Mr. Yashwant?'

Yashwant was somewhat taken aback at this sudden reference to his experiencing pain. He did not reply.

Dilawar Khan continued, 'I know you have not. You are from that part of society which sees all good, does all good, knows all good and believes in all good. Unfortunately, I am not. I am from that unknown section of society which sees all bad, does all bad and believes in all bad only. And we are like that... We can't be changed now.'

Yashwant's sharp mind noted the change from 'I' to 'we' in his last sentence. So, Dilawar Khan was unknowingly talking about the other members in his gang. As a jailor, Yashwant's prime responsibility was to dig out as many details as possible about the criminal's gangs. He sensed an opportunity here.

Dilawar Khan suddenly paused as if he had woken up from slumber and said, 'But why am I telling you all this? These are all my problems. You have nothing to do with this. You keep doing your duty, which currently requires you to take care of me as long as I am in your custody. Goodbye.'

Yashwant had never been turned away like this by anyone in his life before. He felt rather insulted and returned to his office.

Later in the day, Yashwant was unsure about whether his 'Powers' were working or not. But one thing was sure, Dilawar Khan had at least spoken sensibly for a few moments with Yashwant. And by looking at his face, Yashwant could make out that he was speaking from his heart. Yashwant was happy that he had finally broken the ring of resistance around Dilawar Khan. However, he also felt an emotion that he was uncomfortable with - he was becoming somewhat sympathetic towards Dilawar Khan. How could one show sympathy to someone who is a dreaded terrorist, however much pain he might have suffered in his early life?

Yashwant continued with the practice of asking his sub-conscious mind to reform Dilawar Khan. He was optimistic that the results were bound to come sooner or later. After all, it was simple logic that small tasks require small efforts while big tasks require big efforts. And any intention of reforming Dilawar Khan was not a small task by any standards.

A week later, Yashwant once again went to the discussion room and started a conversation with Dilawar Khan. This time, half surprisingly and half expectedly, Dilawar Khan was much more open than ever before. He narrated the story of his childhood and formative years to Yashwant. While listening to him, Yashwant came to understand the probable reasons why Dilawar Khan had become a terrorist, and also learnt many unknown details about the terrorist organisations.

Dilawar Khan was one of six children, who were raised in abject poverty by his parents. His father worked as a construction labourer while his mother worked as part-time maid in other's homes throughout the day to earn money for their survival. The elder children in the family took care of the younger ones when the parents were away at work. There was no proper food or medication available to them and the unhygienic conditions were appalling in the house. Education was a distant dream for them. By default, they were destined to join their father as labourers when they grew older.

However, Dilawar Khan was a rebel from when he was a child. He always questioned the reasons for their poverty. When he saw a car passing by, he would hate the people sitting inside the car. Whenever he saw people entering big hotels, he used to hate them too. His logic was simple: when there were so many people suffering in poverty, how could some people display their wealth in this manner? According to him, these people were insensitive to other's sufferings and had no right to live in society. And therefore, he wanted to teach them a lesson.

Soon, he started targeting these rich people by picking their pockets, or stealing their bags, snatching their chains etc. In the process he made some friends who came from similar backgrounds and also learnt tricks on escaping from the crime scene as soon as possible without leaving a trace of his identity. It was only a matter of time before he started keeping a sharp knife in his pocket. He initially kept it for self defence, but soon started using it for not only threatening but also injuring people when they resisted. He became a notorious figure in the area.

On a festive occasion, Dilawar Khan had asked his father for new clothes. His father was already under stress, earning a meagre amount of money, and he could not afford new clothes for Dilawar. Moreover, Dilawar was not the only child; he would have to buy new clothes for all six children if they had to celebrate the festival. That day was a turning point; Dilawar was totally dejected and decided to chart his own path. He was a teenager with a medium build, strong personality and strong will. He went out with his friends and was plotting new schemes, when they happened to see a weapon shop. They decided to upgrade themselves to a new level by buying these weapons and were contemplating how to raise money to buy them. It was at this juncture that some bearded men found them and asked whether they were ready to work for them. Initially Dilawar and his friends thought that these people were offering them some jobs in a construction site or an agricultural field. They agreed hesitantly, as they needed the money first, irrespective of the source from which it came from. Dilawar sent a message through someone to inform his parents that he was going on a trip with his friends and would return after a few days.

Dilawar and his two friends were taken in an open Jeep to a mountainous area which looked like an army camp. There he observed groups of people engaged in physical activity. Some were getting trained in martial arts, others were learning to climb a 10-meter rope; some were learning to run a few steps over a narrow plank that was placed at a height of four meters and was six meters in length and 8 inches wide; another group was crawling on the floor with weapons in rucksacks on their back etc.

Dilawar was thrilled to see all this. His animal instincts rose to the fore. He was seeing physical action there and also thrilled that he would be equipped with weapons which could harm others and be taught these skills in a professional manner.

Dilawar did not tell his parents about his whereabouts. His parents also apparently did not bother much, and assumed that wherever he was, he must have been happy. Within three months of joining the camp, Dilawar was declared as one of the fastest learners and was entrusted with leading small groups that carried out bomb attacks. He was surprised to see how they made bombs using commonly available daily use items like soap detergents, pins and small ball bearings. It was his nature to take risks in life. As a result, he started liking his work because it was high risk. Every assignment had its own risks and challenges. Over a period of time, he became a good planner as well. He realised that good planning was essential for successfully executing any work. And perfect planning required a good study of the people involved, as well as the place of execution and the specific risks associated with that place, like nearby police stations, whether it was a VIP route etc.

The camp was managed by a tall old man known as Bakhtawar. The people in the camp referred to him as 'Boss' while conversing with him, or while referring to him in their conversations. No one knew his background or any other details. What everyone knew was that he was a very powerful person with many political connections. His influence spread as far as America and Russia apart from the Middle East. Apparently, the Americans had nurtured him to fight with the Russians and had used him successfully for quite some time. Subsequently, after his organisation became strong and had spread its presence to almost every troubled country, the Americans started becoming wary of his powers and wanted to cut his wings. It was then that he started venting his ire on the Americans. At that time, he was shuttling between Afghanistan and Pakistan. He spent most of his time in the hilly areas near the border between these two countries. He had several types of communication devices like radio sets, satellite radio sets and mobile phones. He never used a SIM card for more than one week, for fear of his phones being tapped. He had some unknown sources of funds through which the money flowed for buying weapons and ammunitions. He appeared very gentle and kind hearted but was very tough from within. Bakhtawar had the uncanny ability to be expressionless. Consequently, while talking to him, it was sometimes difficult to know whether he was happy or unhappy while listening to some reports. People also said that he was short tempered, but Dilawar never saw him losing his temper.

Seeing Dilawar's potential to learn quickly, Bakhtawar put him through the more advanced courses that involved the usage of computers for identifying locations using Google Maps, locating GPS Coordinates of a target etc. At times Dilawar wondered, without any formal higher education beyond school level, how he was able to work so skilfully on computers. So, did it mean that working on computers did not require any higher level of knowledge?

Dilawar carried out several bomb blasts during the next five years across various countries like Afghanistan, Yemen, Chechnya, Pakistan, and Sri Lanka, besides India. So, his name was already on the list of wanted terrorists in various countries. He had developed a special skill of being able to change his appearance and disguise himself in a very short time. He always carried several sets of 'faces' with him. These sets of faces comprised different hairstyles, glasses, moustaches and beards. He had the exceptional capability of changing his appearance in a matter of seconds by combining all these to give him an entirely different look.

Apart from this, he also had two flat rubber pieces, which when placed inside the mouth between the teeth and the cheeks at different positions gave an appearance of a round face, a vertical face or an oval face. Finally, there were some small transparent plastic tapes which he used to stick on his ears, stretching them to give a different appearance of flat ears, pulled up ears or round ears.

With this apparatus, he could create over 20 different 'faces'. The makeup looked so genuine that no one ever doubted his appearance. He had used these kits in different combinations at various times. He used them especially when he was required to be at the crime scene for a while before disappearing from there. Accordingly he would stand among the crowd in disguise after committing the crime and then slowly walk away without anyone suspecting him.

Dilawar Khan was speaking for almost two hours describing his past to Yashwant. It was as if he was desperately looking to open up in front of someone and he had found the right person to speak to. For a moment, it appeared as though an aggrieved person was talking to his friend and not a prisoner talking to a jailor. However, once Yashwant came to know all these details through Dilawar Khan, he felt even more responsible. He was not sure how and why Dilawar Khan had chosen to narrate his past in a story-like fashion to Yashwant. Was there any plan behind this? Or were the mystic powers of his sub-conscious mind at work?

He did not know.

However, over the next three weeks, Yashwant went to meet Dilawar Khan in the discussion chamber at least seven times and they had discussions on various subjects. What Yashwant could make out was that Dilawar Khan had become a terrorist due to frustration and helplessness. So, in a way, the government and society were equally responsible for his becoming a terrorist. Unfortunately, the politicians of many developing countries forget that nothing is more dangerous than the anger of a frustrated youth. If a society has large numbers of uneducated and unemployed youth, a revolution is bound to happen sooner or later. When the revolution happens in isolation, people like Dilawar Khan become terrorists, and when it happens on a large scale, it becomes like the Arab Spring of 2011. This is why developing and underdeveloped countries have many more youth becoming terrorists in comparison to developed countries. The small numbers of terrorists found in developed countries are mostly either psychopaths or mentally challenged people.

And after almost two months, observing Dilawar Khan's docile behaviour, Yashwant relaxed the security to some extent. He reduced the number of security guards around his cell. He gave Dilawar access to a slightly larger area outside his small cell. Now he could move around the common area just outside the cell, which was adjoining four other cells. However, Dilawar used that access to only to walk around to thwart his boredom. After all, his well built body needed some physical exercise as well, otherwise it would sag soon.

And observing his good behaviour for almost another three months, Yashwant allowed Dilawar to move around the entire premises inside the jail. Dilawar would normally spend time in gardening activities or helping others in doing their tasks. Yashwant was very happy to see his powers working. So, he was almost successful in reforming Dilawar Khan. It also meant that all Dilawar Khan's future crimes would be avoided. Yashwant continued with his 'Visualisation' regarding reforming Dilawar Khan and that he would not harm anyone.

At times, Yashwant and Dilawar Khan had afternoon tea together in Yashwant's office. On these occasions he used to inspire Dilawar Khan to lead a better life by giving up crime. He would impress upon his mind that a life of honesty and simplicity was far better than what he had lived all these years. Over a period of time Yashwant informed Dilawar Khan that he had been practicing the theory of using the power of sub-conscious mind for the past few months. He also informed Dilawar that he had been testing it on reforming Dilawar Khan for some time now and that he was very satisfied with the results attained thus far. The terrorist listened to Yashwant with keen interest and felt grateful that he was doing so much to reform him.

One day, a new prisoner, Shakeel was brought inside the central prison. Apparently, he had attempted an unsuccessful bank robbery. Shakeel had ambushed the security guard around midnight and hit him hard on his head. He had assumed that the security guard was unconscious after he had hit him; however, the guard was not actually hurt. He had just acted as though he had fainted and at an opportune moment, he swiftly closed the entrance door and alerted the police. The police had no difficulty in catching Shakeel.

That evening, when Dilawar was strolling in the garden, Shakeel came along and smiled at him. Dilawar smiled back without recognising him. It was his routine practice these days to meet and greet all the prisoners, old and new.

Shakeel looked around furtively and whispered to Dilawar, 'I have been sent here by the Boss to free you. I have come up with a scheme. You will be free by next week. There are assignments lined up for you outside.'

Dilawar was stunned. He did not know whether to believe him or not. He could have been a person sent by Yashwant just to check Dilawar's real intentions. Dilawar acted as though he was surprised and said innocently, 'Who is this Boss? And who are you? I don't understand anything you said…'

Shakeel again glanced around furtively and said, 'Dilawar, believe me. I have been sent here only to release you. We shall work out a plan soon…'

Dilawar said, 'Okay, assuming you are sent by the Boss or whoever it is, how you would prove it?'

Shakeel said in a low voice, 'Remember the bomb blasts in Chechnya carried out by you? I had sent the material to you on your address in that villa in suburban area of the city. And that hit and run case in Yemen? I had arranged the local support for you one month before the strike…'

Now Dilawar was sure that Shakeel had indeed been sent by the Boss to rescue him. He too looked around cautiously and said in a low voice, 'Great. I have been waiting for this moment. This innocent jailor Yashwant thinks that I am being reformed by some of his strange powers. It is so easy to fool him. I acted very well during the last few months and he is beginning to feel that I am an absolutely harmless person now. I pity him for believing that a hardcore terrorist like me can be reformed within a few months!'

Chapter 5

Yashwant was very happy that he had almost transformed Dilawar into a helpful and simple person. He praised himself for using his counselling powers and also the mysterious powers of his sub-conscious mind for making this change happen. Now his next plan was to ask for Dilawar Khan's early release from jail. Because, Yashwant felt that there was no point in keeping a reformed person in the jail. Prisons are places of solitary confinement, meant to ensure that the criminals do not continue with their crimes and that society is safe from these people. It was the duty of the prison administration to ensure that criminals are well taken care of and every attempt is made to reform them so that they realise their past mistakes and do not repeat them in the future again. Once the prison authorities are sure that a criminal has changed for the better and does not pose any threat to society, he should be given a chance to live his life all over again. If he is kept in prison for longer periods, then he may lose interest in his life. After all, life is very precious and you only live once; even if there is another life, little is known about that. Hence, one must make every attempt to ensure that this one life is lived as happily as possible. And being in charge of the prison, Yashwant wanted to ensure that the 'reformed Dilawar Khan' lived the remaining part of his life well.

With these thoughts, he came to the office one day and was going through his daily log book when he received a call from Nandakumar. After initial greetings, Nandakumar asked, 'Yashwant, are there any indications of any trouble from within the prison to create any sort of trouble? I mean to harm or help Dilawar Khan? Because, we have been on high alert ever since we shifted Dilawar Khan to your prison a few months back and since then there have not been any secret interceptions by Intelligence Services about any possible specific attack from outside. It is apparently safer from the outside. What about inside?'

Yashwant said confidently, 'Sir, no problem inside too. I have used extensive counselling on Dilawar Khan to ensure that he is reformed. And I am happy to inform you that his behaviour has totally changed compared to what it had been when he was brought here. He is now very sober. He talks to everyone very politely…'

Nandakumar suddenly interrupted him, 'What did you say? He talks to everyone politely? With whom he is allowed to talk?'

Yashwant suddenly felt caught. He replied, 'Sir, by observing his improved behaviour, we have relaxed his security over the last few weeks and now he is allowed to move inside the prison with some relaxed restrictions. And we have observed that he talks to everyone very politely and tries to help everyone.'

Nandakumar almost shouted, 'What nonsense! Don't you remember that he is one of the most dangerous terrorists? Why did you relax his security? Who gave you the permission for doing that? Who will be responsible if something happens to him?'

Yashwant said calmly, 'Sir, sorry, I did this at my own risk. However, I did this only after I tested him in various discussions, and after hearing his views on various subjects. I relaxed his security only after I was fully convinced that he was a changed person and would not harm anyone. Sir, I am responsible for his safety and the safety of others inside the prison. Don't worry…'

Nandakumar was speechless. He said doubtfully, 'Are you by any chance believing in your 'Power of Sub-

Conscious Mind Theory' and relying on your biased observations just to prove the theory correct to yourself?'

Yashwant beamed. 'Yes sir. In fact, I believe that the real force behind Dilawar Khan's reformation is my sub-conscious mind's power. I have been 'Ordering' my sub-conscious mind since I completed my course, to make positive changes in Dilawar Khan and that he should not harm anyone in the future. And I am already seeing the results.'

Nandakumar had neither attended any course on this subject nor did he believe in this theory. He said irately, 'Yashwant, have you gone mad? I am surprised to see that you believe in that theory to such an extent that you are risking even letting a dreaded terrorist mingle with others inside your prison. I hope you are in your full senses when you speak like this. Because, this theory of the sub-conscious mind is still not proven. The people who get trained in it are fascinated by the theory. They practice it. Some of them see good results while some do not. It is not a sure-shot theory guaranteeing you results every time.'

'Sir, I have full confidence and belief that this theory does work,' said Yashwant. 'Whoever practices it correctly will see the results. I could see the results even in my daily life for small insignificant things...'

Nandakumar interrupted, 'Yashwant, small things in daily life are different. And they could have been a coincidence as well. But here you are talking about a terrorist who is a mass murderer. Is your sub-conscious mind so powerful as to alter his mindset and make him a gentleman?'

Yashwant said emphatically, 'Yes sir. I know what I am doing and I take full responsibility for all my actions.'

'Ok, Yashwant,' Nandakumar said. 'I don't know what to say, but please do not put it on record anywhere in official documents that you have tried practicing this theory on Dilawar Khan and that you have got good results. Tomorrow, it could go against you if something goes wrong. It may go on to prove that you have shown negligence of duty.'

Yashwant said, 'Ok sir.' And the conversation ended.

For a moment, Yashwant was lost in deep thought. Was he doing the right thing by relaxing Dilawar Khan's security? Was there any threat to/from Dilawar Khan inside the prison? He had no answers. He only had faith… a strong belief that his theory had worked and Dilawar Khan was reformed. Now, no power could supersede the power of his sub-conscious mind and make changes in his plans. He believed that he had to be right!

Yashwant was now determined that he would ensure that Dilawar Khan was given another chance to rehabilitate himself. It was also the first major victory of his sub-conscious mind. But after his conversation with Nandakumar, he was not very sure how he was going to take this case forward. In fact, he had planned to send a written application to the senior authorities requesting them to consider setting Dilawar Khan free, as he was now reformed. But he was not going to send the application now, because the Government apparently did not believe in 'reformed people'. Surely not the ones reformed through exercising the power of sub-conscious mind of someone else, that too done purely on experimental basis.

Yashwant did believe that if a person has committed crime, then he should face appropriate punishment. But if the crime was committed because of extraneous circumstances, then the person should be pardoned. And in this case, Yashwant was of the opinion that since Dilawar Khan was raised in poverty, without any proper education and basic amenities in life, it was the circumstances that had made him a terrorist. Therefore, he was bent upon giving Dilawar Khan a chance to prove his good side to the world.

While his mind was engrossed in these thoughts, a strange thought came to his mind. What if he let Dilawar Khan escape from the prison? He shuddered at the thought of the disrepute which it would bring to him, but then this would result in meeting his personal objective of seeing Dilawar Khan outside the prison as a reformed man. If Yashwant managed to work it out cleverly, he may not be punished for this lapse, as he would make it appear like an accident or an incident. His direct involvement in the escape drama would not be evident, if he took all the necessary precautions. He suddenly remembered his conversation with Nandakumar and the fact that Nandakumar was now aware of the soft corner Yashwant had towards Dilawar Khan. Would Nandakumar see through Yashwant's secret plan? He did not know. But one suggestion given by Nandakumar was very important, and this would help Yashwant stay away from any suspicion or doubt. And that suggestion was to ensure that there was no record available anywhere, in which Yashwant would note Dilawar Khan's positive behaviour.

After deep thought, Yashwant almost decided that he was going to let Dilawar Khan escape from the prison. At one point he wondered whether Dilawar Khan would escape, if allowed to go. Because he appeared so righteous that he may stick to high moral grounds and refrain from escaping even when an opportunity arose. Now that would be an altogether different situation. But in either case, Yashwant would be a winner. If Dilawar Khan escaped, Yashwant would be thrilled to see that a reformed person had got an opportunity to lead a new life. And if he did not walk out, then he would know that Dilawar Khan was so well reformed that he did not want to avoid his legitimate punishment. There was one gray area though, in this proposition. Assuming that Dilawar Khan escaped from prison, how long could he avoid being caught again by the police? Would he be able to live a clean life in disguise in some remote corner of the world?

With these thoughts, Yashwant went for rounds inside the prison. He found Dilawar Khan and Shakeel in the lawn working with a lawn mower. They were sweating in the sun but still continued to work. Yashwant was overwhelmed with emotions to see that while many other prisoners avoided their tasks, these two were working hard even in the hot afternoon.

Yashwant went near them and asked, 'How are you guys?'

They had spotted Yashwant approaching them. So, they kept quiet while working. Actually they were discussing their modus operandi on how they were going to escape from the prison.

Dilawar Khan said in a humble voice, 'Fine sir. We are ok. This small patch of the garden was remaining to be worked upon, and we were just finishing it. The garden looks so beautiful when the grass is properly trimmed and the bushes are pruned…it pleases the eyes so much.'

Yashwant said, 'Yes, of course. Nature's beauty is there for everyone to see. But very few notice and appreciate it. I am glad that you have developed that vision where you can see this nature's splendour and relish it.'

They kept working on their task. Yashwant was wondering whether he should tell Dilawar Khan that he was going to set him free soon. But he wanted to give him a surprise whenever he did so. And he wanted to watch the expression of gratitude on Dilawar Khan's face when he told him the news. He wanted to caution him about the outside world and to give him a word of advice on how to lead an honourable life. But he felt it was not the right moment. He left from there appreciating the honesty of these two prisoners.

As soon as Yashwant left the scene, Shakeel asked Dilawar Khan, 'Do you think he heard about our plans?'

Dilawar Khan replied, 'No. He was quite far when we switched the topic. And currently he is also blinded by my good behaviour. So, even if he had heard us, he would have thought that we are discussing about some old story or so.'

Dilawar asked Shakeel, 'So, what is the plan? How are we going to escape? Are there any specific instructions from the Boss?'

Shakeel replied, 'Yes, the Boss is coming out with a plan soon. He has kept a tab on everything that is happening inside the prison. He knows that the jailor is mighty pleased with your good behaviour. He wants to make use of the relaxed security to execute the escape plan.'

Dilawar Khan felt sorry for Yashwant. He wondered how Yashwant would feel when he escaped from the prison.

He asked Shakeel, 'And what about the tasks for me? You have any idea about them?'

'As you are aware, our Organisation keeps everything a close secret and only the people who are directly involved in the execution of the plan are provided with information, that too only the Information required to execute the task. However, I overheard them saying that they were planning to kill a prominent builder from South Mumbai as, of late, he has been refusing to give the regular 'hafta' to our Organisation. Other than this I do not know, but this seems to be the priority task which they have kept reserved for you.'

Dilawar Khan was an expert marksman. He was well trained to operate all types of revolvers and machine guns.

Whenever any new model of a weapon was available in the underworld market, Dilawar Khan was trained to use it. He felt happy that he would be out of jail soon.

Yashwant was extremely happy with his 'Achievement': that of reforming Dilawar Khan completely. He felt it was evident from the fact that he had let Dilawar Khan move freely inside the prison for the past few weeks, but he never attempted to escape. As a result, he was going to recommend to the Government that they take a bold new initiative in reforming criminals, by releasing Dilawar Khan early on the grounds of good behaviour. And what could be a better occasion than to announce it on Independence Day, which was celebrated every year with fervour and enthusiasm in the jail. Yashwant had made it a practice to celebrate Independence Day with many prisoners participating in various cultural programs. Various competitions were held, starting almost a week before Independence Day. These included indoor sports like Chess and Carom and outdoor activities like races, long jump, high jump etc. All the prisoners were thrilled to participate in these activities as it gave them a chance to showcase their capabilities. Even though they were criminals, they were human beings too, and they enjoyed these activities.

However, this time, Yashwant was planning one more surprise element for the prisoners. When the National Anthem was played and the flag hoisting done, a helicopter would swoop down and shower flowers all over the ground and on the attendees of the programme. Yashwant had wanted to do this for years but had been unable to do so. This year, he was happy that he had obtained approvals from the necessary authorities including the Civil Aviation and Home Ministry for this new surprise for the prisoners.

When Yashwant went on his rounds he was tempted to reveal to Dilawar Khan that thanks to his good behaviour, he was planning to request the Government for his early release, on Independence Day. However, he did not mention it, as he wanted to see the pure joy on Dilawar Khan's saintly face, when he would announce it from the stage during the programme.

It was still one week to the Independence Day. One day Shakeel hurriedly came looking for Dilawar Khan. He told Dilawar Khan, 'I got the information from the Boss regarding your escape plan.'

Dilawar Khan's eyes sparkled with excitement.

Shakeel said, 'Apparently, Yashwant has organised a helicopter for showering flowers all over the ground after the flag hoisting. We shall use that helicopter to escape.'

Dilawar Khan said, somewhat confused, 'But why would that helicopter help us to escape? That is a police helicopter…'

Shakeel gave a cunning smile. 'Yes, it is a police helicopter, which will be hijacked by our people. Recently we have recruited one of the police staff, Rajan into our Organisation. He is actually fed up with the police department because of the high level of bureaucracy and low wages. He is interested in real action involving high risk activities like run, chase, hide and seek etc. But he is not getting many opportunities due to the political compulsions and is frustrated. We had caught him in one of our encounter scenes and thereafter we let him go back just to work for us. Since he works in the police department, he gives us all the sensitive information about their plans, their secrets and their weaknesses. We pay him much more than what the police department pays him. He is happy and we are also happy. Apparently, in his academy training days, he had taken some flying classes and is a licensed pilot as well. He has been assigned to fly this helicopter. He provided us all this information.'

Dilawar Khan was shocked. He knew the extensive reach of the Boss and his men, but this was too much!

Shakeel continued, 'The plan is like this…the helicopter descends, more than normal, for showering the flowers. When it does so, it will also throw a rope ladder down at right moment and we cling on to that. Before anyone knows, we will be gone. If the plan is executed properly, it would take us around 12 to 13 seconds to do this and we hope that the police do not react faster than that by shooting at us. Even if they succeed in shooting at us, our chances of surviving are very high, because a moving target, both in height and distance, is difficult to shoot at with precision. It would be more difficult because no one would be prepared for this kind of a situation. So, they would take at least around 5-6 seconds to realise what is going on and then reach for their weapons in another 2-3 seconds. That gives us a lead time cushion of around 7-9 seconds. And in that time, our helicopter would have moved a few hundred meters, making it extremely difficult for them to aim and shoot. That's it.'

Dilawar Khan was thrilled at this plan. So, he was going to escape from the prison on the Independence Day. What an irony! Both Dilawar Khan and Shakeel walked down to the parade ground, where the Independence Day function was to be held, to see and assess how the helicopter would come and they started visualising themselves hanging on to the rope ladder and flying high…

For the first time, Dilawar Khan felt that he was not doing the right thing by breaking the trust and faith imposed in him by Yashwant. He remembered those many sessions when Yashwant had come to Dilawar Khan's cell and taught him moral values. The essence of Yashwant's teaching was very simple. Every person who comes into this world has two choices in front of him in almost every situation he faces. Either he can choose to be good, or he can choose to be bad. And these series of decisions determine his past, his present and also his future. In Dilawar Khan's case, all the decisions made by him so far in his life, including the one he was planning to execute on Independence Day, were absolutely bad decisions. These decisions only continued to reinforce his image in society as an offender and a criminal. Yashwant had told him that he could reverse all that by making continuous efforts to be good for a long time. By thinking and doing good over a period of time, a person can actually become good, irrespective of how bad he had been in his past.

Dilawar Khan wondered whether Yashwant would stop being good once he escaped from prison. This was because, in all probability, Yashwant's faith in goodness and noble values would be totally shattered. He would possibly not trust anyone in his life again, especially criminals. Would he stop all the welfare measures initiated by him inside the prison for the benefits of the prisoners? Dilawar Khan had no idea. But one thing was for sure: Yashwant would be crestfallen.

Chapter 6

Finally D-Day arrived. It was a day when two simultaneous plans were going on in the minds of two people. One plan was about goodness, about optimism, about positive thinking, about belief in the powers of the sub-conscious mind to reform a criminal. The other plan was about treachery, about fallen human values, about rebellion, about destruction. The next few hours would decide who wins the day.

The festive mood had set in among all the prisoners. The prize winners of all the weeklong competitions were obviously happier than the others, as they were to receive prizes on the dais from the Chief Guest. There is a child hidden in every person and the child surfaces at every possible opportunity. It was this child within the winners which was making them look forward eagerly to the Independence Day celebration function and more importantly, the prize distribution ceremony.

Dilawar Khan and Shakeel had discussed the plan in detail. They were going to stand near the flagpole so that they could hang on to the rope ladder as quickly as possible. It was a risky exercise and any wrong move would result in widespread shooting by all the security personnel present on the scene. When there are several bullets being fired by several people from all possible directions, the chances of at least one bullet hitting you were very high. One bullet on any sensitive spot on the body like the heart, liver or the forehead was enough to kill a person. Even if it hits the hands and the grip on the rope ladder was momentarily weakened, the fall from such a height was quite likely to be fatal. So, there was no scope for any error in the execution of the plan.

The programme started off with a colourful dance competition. Several groups danced to the latest Bollywood songs in totally innovative ways. Then the drama competition took place in which various teams presented skits on divergent themes including patriotism, the freedom struggle and growth & development of the country. Everyone was in a very festive mood. Yashwant was very happy that the programme was unfolding exactly as he had wished. He was now waiting for the last item of the programme, which was the showering of flowers on the ground by a helicopter. Dilawar Khan and Shakeel were also eagerly waiting for the same event.

Finally the moment arrived. The Chief Guest walked up to the flag pole and stood in position for the flag hoisting. Yashwant was looking proudly at the Indian flag. He was expecting the helicopter at any moment now, as the flowers from the helicopter were to be showered immediately after the flag was hoisted and the flowers fell from inside the flag, once it was unfurled at the top. Dilawar Khan and Shakeel were also eagerly looking forward to this for their great escape.

And then the helicopter appeared on the horizon. The moment was drawing near. The helicopter came close till it was near the flag pole. Then it showered the entire ground with flowers. Yashwant was very satisfied with this plan of celebrating Independence Day in this unique and innovative fashion. As the helicopter stopped briefly near the flag pole, a 15-meter rope ladder descended from its lower compartment to a height at which it could be caught by a person of average height standing on the ground. And before Yashwant or the Chief Guest realised what was happening, Dilawar Khan started running towards the rope ladder and quickly latched on to it by jumping off the ground. The pilot and Dilawar Khan looked down towards Shakeel. Shakeel also came running towards the rope ladder but slipped on his way and he fell down onto the ground. As Shakeel fell down, people surrounded him initially to lift him up, but then to catch him, as it appeared by then that he was also a part of this daring escape act. Dilawar Khan had two options in front of him: either he waited for Shakeel to come, or he left Shakeel there. And as calculated earlier, every second was important. The police would start firing at Dilawar Khan soon from all directions.

Dilawar Khan instantly decided to leave Shakeel there, and signalled the pilot to fly off fast. The helicopter sped away. The police and security forces did fire some shots at the helicopter and Dilawar Khan, but all the bullets missed them, a few of them narrowly.

Now Shakeel was surrounded and immediately overpowered by the security personnel. At first there was confusion among the other prisoners and they had assumed that Shakeel had run towards the helicopter to stop Dilawar Khan from escaping. But very soon, they realized that he was a part of the plan and because he fell down unexpectedly, he could not flee. Now Shakeel was in a fix. He would be questioned about the plan and the planners.

Yashwant was crestfallen. He could not believe that Dilawar Khan had actually escaped from the prison. He had reformed Dilawar Khan and had been confident about his good behaviour. In fact, he had planned to announce in a few minutes that he was recommending leniency for Dilawar Khan to reduce his jail term. He had also planned to sing praises of Dilawar Khan for mending his ways and then urge the other prisoners to look at Dilawar Khan as their role model. After all, it was a difficult task to reform a hardcore criminal.

The news of this daring jail break spread rapidly through the media and Yashwant became the butt of all jokes. He was severely criticised for his laxity in protecting and safeguarding the terrorist under captivity. No one knew whether Dilawar Khan would be captured again and how many days it might take to do so.

In the meanwhile, the police and security forces started tracking the helicopter, which apparently went over the Arabian Sea. They had been unable to chase the helicopter and had watched helplessly as it disappeared.

Yashwant was getting calls after calls from his seniors, the Police Commissioner, the Home Minister, the Media and everyone. He had no answers for them. He had still not recovered from the rude shock.

What worried him was also the apparent fact that his favourite theory of 'the power of sub-conscious mind' had failed him very badly. He had ordered his sub-conscious mind to reform Dilawar Khan. He had asked his powers to see that no one should be harmed by Dilawar Khan ever in the future. Unfortunately, his dreams were crumbling down with this one act of Dilawar Khan. So, had Dilawar Khan only been acting like a reformed person all along? That meant that he had been making a fool of Yashwant all these days, by appearing to have been reformed. How could he do that? Yashwant had no answers to these uncomfortable questions.

That evening, as usual, Yashwant went into his study room and tried to focus on his sub-conscious mind's powers. He started wondering whether all this was a farce. He started doubting whether something like 'the Power of the Sub-Conscious Mind' existed at all. But then, he had been getting so many indications about it being genuine earlier, before he started his master experiment on reforming Dilawar Khan. So, was it that the power worked for usual routine things, but was rendered helpless while dealing with some strong-minded people? Or was it that every person could use the power of the sub-conscious mind only up to limit, beyond which it fails him?

On the other hand, his positive mind frame was telling him that this theory did work. The power of the sub-conscious mind does exist and there is no limit for it, because it draws its energy from the limitless infinite powers of Nature. Sometime, the results may come sooner and sometimes later, but results do come. And…that rang a bell in his mind. It was as if he had been searching for an answer and finally got it after a long thought process during which, at some moments he was close to getting an answer. So, was it possible that his sub-conscious mind was actually working, while the results would be seen sometime in the future? But, Dilawar Khan had already escaped from prison. What good could it have done? How would it have complied with Yashwant's directives to the sub-conscious powers that Dilawar Khan gets reformed and that he does not harm anyone?

Well…only time would tell whether the powers of the sub-conscious mind were really at work or not...

The helicopter went well past the shores and deep into the sea, where a fishing boat was ready to take Dilawar Khan safely back to Mumbai in a different get-up. The boat had 10 fishermen and Dilawar Khan became the eleventh. There was a makeup kit on the boat which transformed him into an authentic looking fisherman wearing a multi coloured shirt and a short lungi. He had a wig which changed his hairstyle, covering most of his forehead, and a slightly thicker moustache extending over his lower cheeks. No one could have identified Dilawar Khan in this attire.

Once on shore, Dilawar Khan was taken in an Ambassador car to a crowded chawl in the Bhendi Bazaar area of Mumbai. One of the rooms in the chawl was rented by one of the inconsequential members of the Organisation. He appeared to be a good, upstanding citizen but provided all the required auxiliary support to the Organisation's members as and when required. Dilawar Khan was provided with a detailed road map of Mumbai city with all the important landmarks. He was advised to stay holed up there till the search operation cooled down. He was specifically instructed not to come out of the room at any cost. An Organisation member met all his food requirements. There was a small TV so Dilawar Khan could watch all the news channels and track the progress of the investigations. The police department appeared to be absolutely clueless about his whereabouts and was wondering whether he had fled to Pakistan in the helicopter. After dropping Dilawar Khan, the helicopter was actually made to land on the helipad of a guest house. This guest house was occasionally used by the Organization to provide temporary hiding places, in the hilly areas of the Ghat section between Mumbai and Pune. The helicopter would not be used in the near future, as it would be identified easily and that could give some leads to the police department. They were contemplating taking the helicopter to Pakistan after a few weeks.

When Dilawar Khan would get bored, he would go out in disguise for a walk in the market area around his building and return. He took special care to ensure that his appearance did not give anyone any clue or raise any doubt about his original identity. After almost one month of confinement in the chawl, Dilawar Khan was given the new assignment. He was ordered to kill the famous builder of South Mumbai, Kripesh Mehta. He was provided all the necessary information about Kripesh including video clips and photographs from various angles, his daily routine, the places where he operated from, the route on which he travelled for his daily work etc. Dilawar Khan always executed his jobs with perfection and hence gathered as much information as possible to ensure that there were no surprises during the execution of the plan.

He found out that Kripesh was a highly successful builder who had developed assets worth crores of rupees in the last 12 years to become a leading developer in Maharashtra and Gujarat. Apparently, there was a dispute regarding his 'protection money' which was increased recently by the Organisation. The Organisation demanded a 40% increase whereas Kripesh had insisted that due to the ongoing recession, the business was dull and he was not making enough money to give that additional sum. This disagreement soon snowballed into a conflict and the Organisation wanted to teach him a lesson. Their point was that if one person defied their orders today, there could be a few more who resisted them tomorrow and that would gradually result in weakening their hold over the market and its players.

Dilawar Khan zeroed in on three/four ways to eliminate Kripesh. One was to visit his office posing as a customer and kill him there. The second was to plan a car accident with a truck, whose driver would run away immediately after the accident to a remote village in Bihar. The third was to intercept him on a road near a traffic signal and shoot him point blank. The fourth was to shoot him from the opposite building through a telescopic gun.

After much thought, he decided to kill Kripesh on a road near a traffic signal, as the chances of him being identified in any CCTV footage were the least in this option. Having decided the modus operandi, he then carefully studied all the routes on which Kripesh travelled regularly and then shortlisted the SVP Road. There were three signals on SVP Road, which was usually a congested road. So, it was very likely that he would be able to get near Kripesh's car on a motor cycle near one of the traffic signals. His plan was to stand close to car from the right side, aim at Kripesh sitting in the rear seat and spray him with bullets. His objective was that at least three bullets should hit him to ensure that he died before receiving medical attention in any nearby hospital. Reaching a nearby hospital through the traffic would require at least 35 minutes. And immediately after spraying the bullets, Dilawar would turn the motorcycle around over the road divider, which was a small 6-inch layer of bricks on that part of SVP Road and then race away from the scene. Of course, he would wear adequate protective gear to conceal his identity like a helmet with a tinted glass covering his face, a windcheater to hide his physique in case people saw him in that frenzy, and hand gloves to hide his complexion. With these precautions, he expected that no one would be able to get any precise details about his personality or identity, which could be traced back to him later on. Thankfully, due to the rising pollution levels in Mumbai, most of the ladies drove their two wheelers with their faces completely covered leaving a small opening for the eyes. So, this would not be an unusual new sight for people. At the most they might think that he was beauty conscious, taking unreasonable care of his complexion.

Dilawar had surveyed all the three signals and all the small lanes leading from the opposite roads near these signals. He even studied where he would abandon the motor cycle with a fake number plate and through which narrow lane he would run to cross two rows of buildings, so that he could appear on another parallel road absolutely without any tension and mingle with the crowd.

Dilawar Khan thought for some time whether it would help him if he took someone along with him on this mission. The companion could sit as a pillion rider and give Dilawar clear control over the target. But later, he cancelled the idea and decided to go it alone.

Having prepared all the ground work and the plan of execution, he was now waiting for final 'go ahead' signal from the Boss to strike...

Chapter 7

Yashwant was extremely distressed at the bold daylight escape of Dilawar Khan via a police driven helicopter. He had not expected this from Dilawar Khan. However, now that this had already happened, he could do nothing about it. All he could do was try and ensure that Dilawar Khan was recaptured at the earliest and tried in a court of law like any other terrorist. As and when he was caught by the police, he would be additionally charged with escaping from prison.

Yashwant was personally monitoring the team interrogating Shakeel to get as many details about Dilawar Khan as possible. It was a blessing for Yashwant that Shakeel could not escape from the prison as he was now a live source of information for Yashwant. Initially Shakeel refused to divulge any information, but from the third day onwards, tired of the harsh conditions which he was subjected to, he started blurting out, one by one, all the Organisation's secrets that he knew. Through sustained interrogation, Yashwant learnt that both Dilawar Khan and Shakeel worked in the same Organisation and worked under the instructions of the Boss. Dilawar Khan's escape was facilitated by the Boss, who operated from outside the Indian borders. He had several operations running in different countries. Except for the fact that all the operations were on wrong side of the law, the way he managed and controlled them was extremely professional.

Like any other corporate entity, there was a proper HR department, which scouted for frustrated youth in developing countries. The recruiting team went to crowded areas and searched for young people with good physiques and offered them 'jobs'. The team was skilled enough to approach the right candidates. Once selected, these people were taken to one of several camps and trained there. There was a proper register with details of all the recruits and their details like joining date, strengths, training imparted etc. There was no salary as such, as it was given based on the specific assignments. All their daily living expenses were met by the Organisation.

Then there was a systematic finance department which managed the finances for all the operations like procuring weapons and ammunitions. The payments were generally made through Hawala transactions, which was a parallel way of transferring money from any part of the world to any other part of the world illegally. No Government could ever detect this type of payment. The payments were also made to different stakeholders for all the logistics involved in planning and execution of the attacks.

There was also a marketing and communication department which constantly prepared and distributed new pamphlets containing somewhat inflammatory matter for flaring the emotions of the people on a wide range of subjects. The most common subjects were related to some regional or local anti-Government opinion. Such matters generally portrayed the local Government in poor light and they were shown as weak minded. This division always kept abreast of unpleasant developments across the world to take benefit of any riots or unrest in any part of the world, as they would then capitalise on those incidents to show that grave injustice was being meted out to some section of the society. They would then invite people to join hands to combat those forces and provide justice to the deprived.

Finally, there was a training division where the new recruits were trained on using various types of weapons. The Organisation had access to all the latest weapons available in the world. Whenever any new model was available, the Organisation received a consignment of those weapons with their instruction manuals and essential spares. The trainees' physical strength and capabilities were developed by conducting regular drills in tough conditions like muddy areas and rocky terrains. This division had a list of premier visiting faculty from secret intelligence agencies of around half a dozen countries including Pakistan and Afghanistan.

Yashwant was astonished with the information he received. He had never imagined that any underworld Organisation could have such a structured method of operations. On interrogating Shakeel further, he realised that it was a well hatched plan by the Organisation to airlift Dilawar Khan from prison on Independence Day. They had successfully fooled the entire police department and snatched away from them their prized possession. Shakeel also revealed that the Organisation planned to kill one of the affluent builders in South Mumbai soon and that Dilawar Khan would be possibly involved in this proposed attack.

This information was enough for Yashwant to start working. He met the police commissioner of Mumbai, Viswanathan and appraised him about the impending plan of the Organisation. They did not know which builder was the target, but it was someone from South Mumbai. So, they carefully took a list of all the builders based in South Mumbai and zeroed in on five builders who were doing good business in spite of the dull business environment. Kripesh was one among them.

Viswanathan then started contacting each one discreetly without giving out any details about the possible threat to their lives, because he was not sure which one among the five was the target and secondly, he did not want to create any panic. After talking to all the five builders he realized that Kripesh was most likely to be on the Organisation's radar because he seemed to be making good money, and also, it appeared that he was in contact with the Organisation. Viswanathan did not have any evidence; it was only a gut feeling.

Viswanathan called Kripesh to a restaurant for a business lunch. They had known each other for a few years now and therefore, there was no reason for Kripesh to wonder about any specific reason for this lunch invitation. After a general discussion on the fluctuating weather conditions, dull business environment, growing traffic menace in Mumbai etc, Viswanathan started the sensitive conversation very cautiously with him. He said, 'Kripesh bhai, by any chance did anyone from the underworld contact you ever in the past for anything?'

Kripesh was startled at this unexpected question and his sudden expressions of surprise-cum-guilt did not miss Viswanathan's sharp eyes. Kripesh cleared his throat and said, 'Well, sometimes they do try to call me and pressurise me, you know. That's it... Nothing else.'

Viswanathan looked at him coldly and said, 'When did they contact you last? Was there any disagreement between you and them recently?'

Now Kripesh became slightly panicky. He said, 'Yes, in fact they were demanding more money and...'

Viswanathan interrupted him, 'That means you were paying them some money, right?'

Kripesh realized that he was now in a trap. He said, 'Yes. I was paying them a fixed amount every quarter as protection money.'

Viswanathan said, 'Why did you not complain to the police about this earlier?'

Kripesh said exasperatedly, 'Even now I am not complaining to you... I don't know how you came to know about this and why you are asking me details on this subject, which I consider is purely personal.'

Viswanathan did not know how to reveal the sensitive information to Kripesh - that his life was under threat from the underworld. He wanted to make Kripesh aware of the danger without frightening him.

Viswanathan said, 'So, where was the disagreement then?'

Kripesh was slowly losing his cool now. He said, 'See, you police have no control over the underworld. They've been operating under your nose for several years now. The people operating in the underworld have changed over the years but their reach is growing wider and wider. We have to care for our safety and you are questioning me why I pay money for ensuring my own safety, which you cannot guarantee me?'

Viswanathan said,' Stop this nonsense Kripesh! Do you know that your life is in danger now because of whatever disagreement you have had over the protection money amount?'

After listening to Viswanathan, fear gripped Kripesh's mind. He was shocked to hear that there was a threat to his life.

Viswanathan continued, 'Kripesh, please calm down and listen carefully. We have got secret information that the terrorist Dilawar Khan, who escaped from prison recently, has been entrusted with an assignment to kill you.'

Kripesh started sweating and his legs were shaking. He was dumbstruck at this news.

He said, 'Viswanathan, please save me. I don't want to die. They were asking me more money and I refused. I tried to convince them that business was dull and that I would continue to pay the same amount for some more time, but they insisted on a hike. I never imagined that they would plan to kill me over this disagreement.'

Viswanathan said calmly, 'Relax Kripesh, we are here to save you. We will do our best to protect you. We also want to arrest Dilawar Khan, who has so brazenly escaped from the prison.'

Over the next two hours, Viswanathan asked Kripesh about all his details like which places he visited frequently, which route he took from home to office and back, the area around his office and home, his staff details etc, to detect and plug any weak points from where Dilawar Khan could strike. And an elaborate plan for providing complete security to Kripesh was worked out.

An enhanced security system around his house and office was provided with immediate effect. The security in-charge was provided with wireless devices for live communication with Viswanathan. The places he visited regularly were kept under close surveillance. Whenever he travelled in his car, an escort team comprising four motorcycles with policemen in civilian clothes would follow him closely. So, while anyone from the police department could see four policemen surrounding Kripesh's car anytime, a laymen would see Kripesh's car surrounded by the traffic on road.

Viswanathan briefed Yashwant about his success in identifying the correct builder from South Mumbai under the scanner of the Organisation and also the measures taken by him to not only save Kripesh but also to nab Dilawar Khan. It was of paramount importance for Yashwant to arrest Dilawar Khan and put him back in the same prison to settle his earlier score. By now Yashwant had lost some of his faith in the power of the sub-conscious mind. However, out of curiosity he wanted to check where he had gone wrong. But then, sometimes he also wondered, had he really gone wrong? He had been ordering his subconscious mind that Dilawar Khan was reformed and that he does not harm anyone. So, till there was enough evidence to suggest that he had harmed someone, maybe it was not right to be doubtful… At these thoughts, he would stop thinking anymore about it, as he felt that it was becoming much too fanciful and assumptive to either believe the theory of the power of the sub-conscious mind or to dismiss it as a gimmick without any concrete facts to conclusively prove or disprove it.

Finally the day arrived when Dilawar Khan was scheduled to kill Kripesh. He woke up as usual and got ready for the task. He wore a black jerkin over his dark shirt in which he could hide his compact modern revolver. His plan was simple. He would wait opposite Kripesh's house near a shop from 8.30am. And as Kripesh came out of his house at his usual time of 9am, to follow him, keeping a distance, till he reached SVP Road. As he entered SVP Road, he would get closer to his car and try to stop near his car at the traffic signal. The act was to be performed when the signal was about to turn green, so that the traffic would start moving and the opposite lane would be empty. It was also desirable to be as close to the traffic signal as possible, so that he could turn around the motorcycle easily.

As planned, Kripesh came out of his house at 9am and headed for his office in his car. Behind his car, Dilawar Khan was riding the motorcycle. Kripesh's car entered SVP Road. Dilawar Khan now started getting closer to the car. There was regular morning traffic on the road. As the first traffic signal appeared, Dilawar Khan wanted to close in on Kripesh's car when suddenly an auto rickshaw came from nowhere and filled the gap parallel to the car. As a result, Dilawar Khan was left a few meters behind the car. That was not good. He had missed his first chance. He had two more traffic signals. He waited patiently appearing very natural and observing the traffic to see if any police vehicle was around. He did not spot any. Slowly the traffic moved on and they reached the second signal.

Here, Dilawar Khan wanted to somehow get his motorcycle close to Kripesh's car. He was almost there, but suddenly another motorcycle entered from his left and stood close to the car. Once again Dilawar Khan had missed the opportunity. He could not strike the target unless he was in range. There was no way he could have moved closer to the car now and he was left with the third and final traffic signal if he had to achieve his goal today. He wondered from where this motorcycle had come and cursed the rider in his mind. He looked at the person with an irritated expression and noticed something. He had seen this motorcycle from the time he had started following Kripesh's car from his house. What a coincidence, he thought. But then suddenly he noticed that there was another motorcycle of the same brand on the other side of the car as well with a number plate almost matching with this motorcycle with a difference in only the last digit. He wondered whether these two motorcycles had been bought simultaneously. And to his horror, he found that there were two more motorcycles just ahead of them on both sides of the car with the same series of number plates. And on closer observation, he noticed that these people appeared to be well built as if they exercised regularly and kept their bodies in great shape, as though they were a part of some commando force, or the police force.

Suddenly Dilawar Khan felt panicky. There was no way that these four motorcycles so close to Kripesh's car, almost surrounding it, were there without any specific purpose. He wondered, whether they had any inkling of his proposed attack on Kripesh? His doubts got further strengthened when he observed that they all moved on together from the second traffic signal and even when there was clear road ahead for a few moments, the motorcycles did not speed past the car. Were they protecting Kripesh? Before they reached and stopped at the third traffic signal, he needed to confirm this point and also take a quick decision whether to go ahead with the plan. There was no point in attempting the plan if there was heavy security protecting the target. That would amount to inviting trouble.

As they moved along to reach the third traffic signal, he observed that the four men on the motorcycles were also silently looking at each other once in a while and indicating something. For some reason, he felt that they were discussing about him. He had almost covered his entire body with his dark coloured outfit, the black jerkin and hand gloves. He had also worn a helmet with tinted glass which covered his face completely. In normal circumstances, people would have looked at him and thought in their minds that he was either much too protective about his skin, or was someone out to do something heroic or someone who wanted to act funny on the road. But he felt that the four motorcycle riders had now taken notice of him, since he too had been following the car for a long distance and time.

Dilawar Khan had to make a quick decision whether he was going to strike irrespective of this newly found security cordon around Kripesh. He remembered that once a task is taken at hand, it has to be accomplished. There was no looking back. This was not acceptable to the Boss. The way he was trained, he was even required to sacrifice his life in order to attain the larger objective of the Organisation. So, was he seeing his death in front of him now? He was on a mission to kill Kripesh. But, would he get killed in the process? Well, anything could happen. The next few seconds were going to decide that.

At the third traffic signal, Dilawar Khan got an opportunity to take his motorcycle right next to Kripesh's car, on the right side. The right side was preferred, as he could take a U-turn immediately after executing the task. He moved his head to the left and saw Kripesh talking on his mobile, gesturing with his hand intermittently. The timer installed at the traffic signal was counting down the time 17…16...15 seconds for turning the red signal to green. His plan was to act when the timer showed 4 seconds remaining for the traffic light to turn green. Because then it would take him 3-4 seconds to fire six rounds at Kripesh and immediately take a U-turn at the traffic signal and speed past the empty road.

The timer showed 6…5…4 seconds and instantly, Dilawar Khan took out his revolver from his jerkin and started firing at Kripesh. While firing the bullets, he noticed that his concentration was diverted because of the four escorts and he was not able to aim precisely. His task was much more complicated because he needed to be superfast in escaping from the scene, as any delay would result in his instant capture and even his immediate death in the impromptu encounter. He also noticed during those few seconds that some bullets did hit Kripesh. However, Dilawar Khan was surprised that while Kripesh appeared to be terrified and shocked, he still did not collapse. Suddenly there was chaos around and the people around started running around helter-skelter leaving their vehicles not knowing what was going on. The security men on the four motorcycles immediately got down from their motorcycles and approached Dilawar Khan to catch him. In a split second, Dilawar Khan suddenly accelerated his motorcycle and turned around at the signal and sped past the empty road in the opposite direction. The four escorts checked Kripesh's condition inside the car and abandoned the idea of following Dilawar Khan. The entire traffic around them was already in disarray with several vehicles around them and it was much too difficult to chase him now.

Immediately, an ambulance was called and they took Kripesh to a nearby hospital.

Dilawar Khan left the motorcycle in a narrow lane 2 km away from the spot and took an auto rickshaw to reach his chawl in Bhendi Bazaar. He settled down in his room and switched on the TV to watch the news. The 'Breaking News' on every news channel said, 'Prominent builder Kripesh Mehta attacked in broad daylight…' However, as the details started pouring in, Dilawar Khan was in for a big shock. Kripesh had survived the attack with some minor injuries. Only one of the six bullets had brushed past his left arm. The remaining bullets had actually hit the bulletproof jacket which Kripesh was wearing at the time of the incident. And soon, the police commissioner Viswanathan appeared at a press conference and claimed that it was actually a victory of the police department. He described how the secret agencies of the police department had acted on a tipoff and investigated the information further to identify the correct person on the radar of the Organisation. He also described how they had beefed up security measures to protect Kripesh's life. It was their timely action that had saved Kripesh's life today. They also confirmed that the attacker was Dilawar Khan, the prisoner who escaped from prison a few months ago. Finally, Viswanathan also committed to the media and through them to the citizens of Mumbai that they would nab Dilawar Khan from wherever he was hiding within the next two days, as they had sealed each and every exit point immediately.

Kripesh's family was very happy to see him alive after the attack on his life. They were very thankful to the police department for their timely action in alerting them so that adequate precautions could be taken to protect Kripesh. Moreover, this incident also emboldened Kripesh and he vowed that he would never pay a single paisa to the underworld in future. He told his colleagues from the builder fraternity, 'Actually we are the people who spoil them. When one of us gives them money out of fear, they are encouraged to ask for money from all others. If all of us are firm on our stand not to pay them, they can't extract money from us anymore like this. The police department is capable of providing us adequate protection whenever we need it. So, let us stand united and eradicate the underworld from Mumbai. Together...we can.' Seeing his enthusiasm and bravado, other builders and affluent businessmen were also inspired to follow along the same lines and live a life free from the shadows of the underworld.

Dilawar Khan called Bakhtawar to give him the report. Bakhtawar operated from Pakistan these days. Dilawar Khan said, 'Boss, sorry… I do not know how this happened… I mean how he escaped his death. I fired all six bullets into him.'

There was a brief silence on the other side and then Bakhtawar said, 'In our Organisation, we have few chances to say sorry and tender our apologies for failures. I am disappointed. We gave you training for so long, for what? To see this kind of result?'

Dilawar Khan did not know what to say. During his training in the camp, his interaction with the Boss was limited. Dilawar Khan had sometimes seen the Boss watching the proceedings on the training ground from a distance. He had spoken to him many times thereafter, but that was always when the Boss was in a good mood after tasks were successfully accomplished. This was the first time that he was speaking to the Boss when he was angry. He had heard that Boss was a short-tempered person and could become hysterical when the desired results were not achieved. Yet, he had also displayed another contrasting facet of his personality while planning and organising attacks, one that was very methodical, balanced and cool.

Dilawar Khan said, 'Boss, I need another chance. Even I do not like to fail. But somehow they seemed to have sensed that we were planning to attack Kripesh. Therefore, they added security for him and also advised him to wear a bulletproof jacket. The presence of those four security guards distracted me while I aimed at Kripesh. If I had sensed earlier that he was wearing a bulletproof jacket, I would have fired on his forehead…'

Bakhtawar said, 'That shows how weak our system has become. We now need to find out how he came to know about our plans. That is very important. A water tank with a leak somewhere will never fill to its brim. Similarly, unless we identify and eliminate the source of their information, we may not be able to strike in the future.'

Dilawar Khan did not know what to say. He said obligingly, 'Yes Boss.'

The Boss continued, 'Did you hear the press conference a few minutes ago? They have also identified that the attacker was you. And they have promised to nab you in the next two days. It is not safe for you to stay there anymore. I shall arrange to shift you to Pakistan in the next two days.'

Dilawar Khan was surprised at this. He said, 'But Boss…'

The Boss interrupted him and said, 'Ok, I don't want to talk anymore now, as our phone could be tapped and even otherwise, after every such attack, the police track and monitor all the calls made to or received from Pakistan. So, don't call me back. Check your email in the evening.' The Boss hung up. Dilawar Khan was lost in his thoughts. So, the arrangements were being made to shift him to Pakistan. The reason given was that he was not safe here.

Was there was any other assignment waiting for him there? Or was the Organisation not willing to take any more risks with him? Did they want to silence him once and for all for his failure? He had heard that in a horse race, when a horse stumbles on the race course, they fire him after the race is over. That horse is never allowed to participate in any race in the future. Was the Boss treating him similarly?

He had no answers.

Yashwant was utterly disappointed with himself to see that Dilawar Khan had managed to escape yet again. He had high hopes on the 'Power of the Sub-Conscious Mind' theory. However, the way things had turned out, it appeared that the theory did not work in reality. So, to clarify his doubts, he went to Yogeshwar one day and asked him, 'Guruji, why didn't the theory work for me? Was there something wrong in the way I practiced it? Or… is there something wrong with me to expect a hardcore criminal to be reformed through this theory?'

Yogeshwar thought deeply for a while and looking straight at Yashwant said, 'What exactly have you been ordering your sub-conscious mind?'

Yashwant was confused with the question. He replied, 'Well, I have been ordering that Dilawar Khan be reformed and that he does not cause harm to anyone in the future.'

Yogeshwar said, 'And are you aware whether he is now reformed or whether he has harmed anyone?'

Yashwant replied, 'Well, I cannot say whether he is reformed or not. But yes, he has escaped from the prison in a daring and adventurous attempt. He tried to kill Kripesh at a traffic signal in broad daylight…'

Yogeshwar interrupted, 'Did he kill Kripesh?'

'Well, no. He tried to kill Kripesh, but because of our intelligence and preparedness, we saved Kripesh's life.'

Yogeshwar asked, 'So, in a way, did he harm anyone?'

Yashwant was getting Yogeshwar's point. He said, 'No. To the best of my knowledge, so far he has not harmed anyone.'

'See Yashwant, the theory of power of sub-conscious mind rarely fails,' Yogeshwar said. 'It fails only when the person does not practice it properly or when he practices it for wrong purposes. The sub-conscious mind derives its power from the supreme forces of Nature and these forces will always support good causes. The world is actually meant to be a good place to live in. All people were originally meant to be good. All human beings were meant to be happy. However, people themselves, through their acts, bring upon themselves misery and unhappiness. Therefore, whenever the sub-conscious mind gets a command to do good to someone, it acts with alacrity and makes that happen.'

Yashwant said, 'So do you mean Guruji that the acts of Dilawar Khan escaping from prison and his missing killing Kripesh were acts of goodness?'

Yogeshwar said, 'Of course. See Yashwant, Dilawar Khan escaped from the prison. It was definitely an unlawful act. However, it could just be that he ran away as per the design of Nature's forces to realise your command to your sub-conscious mind. Maybe he is destined to save a few lives by being outside jail rather than by being inside it. As regards his missing to strike Kripesh, it is surely because of your sub-conscious mind's powers. They intervened and ensured that none of the six bullets struck him so as to cause him any harm. Just imagine, if any one bullet had struck him on the forehead, it could have been fatal.'

Yashwant was now even more confused. One part of his mind was accepting the argument put forth by Yogeshwar while the other part was not. He was wondering whether it was right for him to still continue believing in the theory when he had already brought so much disrepute to himself within the police department.

However, after deep thought, he decided to continue with his prayers about ordering his sub-conscious mind to reform Dilawar Khan and to see that he does not harm anyone. That evening, he also wondered whether his intermittent thoughts about releasing Dilawar Khan had been picked up by his sub-conscious mind. He had not actually *visualised* that Dilawar Khan had been released from the prison, but *did think* about it many times. So, did his sub-conscious mind pick up his involuntary thoughts also, apart from taking instructions through his conscious orders? If that were so, was it good or bad? If it was true, then he would have to be extremely careful even in thinking about anything, as it could be picked up by his sub-conscious mind for execution.

The next day, he went to Viswanathan's office to see how their efforts were going on to nab Dilawar Khan. Viswanathan was quite optimistic and said, 'We have already spread out our teams on ground to nab him. We have tracked the route on which he fled the crime scene and the entire area is now being combed by us to see where he is hiding. We have cordoned off the entire area in four localities where we strongly suspect that he is hiding. Our investigations so far reveal that he is most likely hiding somewhere in the Bhendi Bazaar area. We are going house to house and asking the residents about any suspicious movements observed by them.'

The police were going almost lane by lane asking people whether they had spotted anyone looking like Dilawar Khan. They had taken his file photo and were showing it to all shopkeepers as well. Their hopes were suddenly rekindled when some people started recognising Dilawar Khan and said that they had seen him moving about in their lane occasionally. Dilawar Khan had been actually very careful and had come out only at odd hours from his room. Still, there were apparently some people who identified him in the photo carried by police.

Dilawar Khan was resting in his room when his phone rang and disturbed him from his momentary sleep. It was the Boss.

Dilawar Khan said, 'Yes Boss…'

'Listen carefully Dilawar, you need to move out of your room as fast as possible,' said the Boss. 'The police is zeroing in on your building based on random enquiries with the residents around your locality in Bhendi Bazaar. They might reach your place anytime soon.'

Dilawar Khan was shocked. He said, 'Boss, but how come? And what if they catch me? I am sure Yashwant would ensure that I get a life term. Where should I go now?'

Boss said, 'You have no time to discuss and decide on this now. Do whatever you can and leave the place. Use the passport sent to you yesterday to travel to Pakistan. It is not safe for you to stay in India anymore.'

Dilawar Khan said, 'Ok Boss…' and hung up. He looked down from the window of his small room on the second floor and found that two policemen were already standing there talking to someone who was looking at the building and gesturing towards the window of his room. So he was in real danger and he needed to act very quickly. He had no time. Since he was an expert in disguising himself at short notice, he quickly donned the disguise of a scavenger by wearing a faded t-shirt and trousers rolled up till knees. He also applied an artificial unkempt beard on his chin and mussed his hair. With his belongings, which were essentially money, passport and some maps, a diary etc, he moved out of his room. As he reached the ground floor, he observed that the two policemen had by then called almost a dozen of their colleagues in anticipation of catching Dilawar Khan and also to be prepared in case he retaliated.

There was only one exit route from the building and the police were spreading themselves around the building and inching towards it. Dilawar Khan came out of the building and started walking with a slight limp in his left leg. He carried his belongings in a dirty bag as if he was carrying trash.

As he passed by the team of policemen, no one took notice of him. However, as he went past them, suddenly one of them asked, 'Hello… Mr….'

Dilawar Khan's heart skipped a beat. He was tense wondering whether they had discovered his identity. He stopped and slowly turned to face them.

One of the police officers said, 'Who are you and what are you doing here?'

Dilawar Khan realised that they were only suspicious about him. So, feeling braver, he said in a hoarse voice, 'Sir, I am the garbage collector here. Doing my duty…'

The police said reluctantly, 'Ok. Ok… Please go…'

Dilawar Khan was relieved and continued walking slowly with the limp. He reached the main road and disappeared from the scene. Now his task was to change his appearance again and reach the airport. He quickly called a taxi and even as the taxi driver looked suspiciously at his unkempt appearance, he said, 'Let us go to airport.' The taxi driver was surprised that a scavenger was asking to go to the airport and thought, that someone should put a full stop to this unhealthy competition among the low cost carriers…what kind of people were travelling by flights these days…

As soon as the taxi started, Dilawar Khan started changing his makeup and clothes in the rear seat. The taxi driver looked at him through the rear view mirror and asked him smilingly, 'Are you an actor, sir?'

Dilawar Khan smiled back at him and said, 'Yes, I am acting as a scavenger in a TV serial. Now I am heading for another assignment and have no time to change.'

The taxi driver just smiled and wondered at the lifestyle of TV artists. He dropped Dilawar Khan at the airport and was quite surprised to see the complete transformation in Dilawar Khan's appearance. He could not believe that the person who got into his Taxi in Bhendi Bazaar and the one getting out of his taxi at the airport were one and the same.

Dilawar Khan walked inside the airport with another identity as per the passport arranged for him by the Boss. He quietly booked a ticket for Islamabad and sat in the waiting lounge. The TV news was flashing with the 'Breaking News' that the police had identified Dilawar Khan's hideout but he had escaped in the nick of time. He was interested in finding out whether they had any clues about him. Apparently they had not yet identified that the scavenger walking past them was him. He thought that once he boarded the plane to Islamabad, he would be safe. The Indian police could not reach him once he took off from Mumbai Airport and landed in Islamabad.

Dilawar Khan sat and watched the news casually without appearing perturbed and as soon as the boarding announcement was made, he proceeded to board the flight. The flight took off as per schedule and Dilawar Khan looked down at Mumbai from his window seat with mixed feeling. He still remembered the 'Reformation Classes' Yashwant had arranged and the trust and faith Yashwant had reposed in him.

No one had shown so much faith in him in the past... not even the Boss.

Chapter 8

Dilawar Khan met Bakhtawar on the third day of his arrival in Islamabad. They met at a nondescript apartment in a crowded area of Islamabad, used by the Organisation for these kinds of short meetings. It was a bit safer to move around in Islamabad, as Bakhtawar had a lot of sway over the local administration. There was a broad level of understanding between the Government, the Military and the Organisation. Generally they respected and cooperated with each other to achieve mutually desirable objectives. However, on the paper, the Organisation was considered as anti Government and the Government kept giving some statements from time to time about taking stern action against the Organisation.

Bakhtawar expressed his concern and disappointment at Dilawar Khan's failure to kill Kripesh. He knew that the police had been able to protect Kripesh only because of the leads provided by Shakeel in jail. But then, leaving Shakeel behind while Dilawar Khan escaped in a helicopter had also been a mistake. Nevertheless, he was happy that Dilawar Khan had escaped from an Indian prison and was safely with him in Pakistan now.

Dilawar Khan said, 'Boss, what next? Any assignment lined up for me?'

Bakhtawar looked thoughtful and said, 'Yes. There is one very sensitive assignment and I wanted only you to handle it. Hence I waited for you to come over here.'

Dilawar Khan was happy to note that the Boss still had some faith in his capabilities and skills. He said, 'Yes Boss, your wish is my command. Please order…'

Bakhtawar said, 'Ever since Khwaja Salahudeen has become the Home Minister, he is bent upon improving the law and order situation in Pakistan. And that is a problem for us…'

Dilawar Khan was listening, wondering what the plan could be to overcome this obstacle.

Bakhtawar continued, 'If he goes on like this, soon the Organisation will close down and we will have to look for jobs. We need to stop him right away.'

Dilawar Khan said cautiously, 'So, Boss, are we planning to eliminate Khwaja Salahudeen?'

Bakhtawar said, 'No, no…not yet. We just want to teach him a lesson. We need his active support for our existence and growth. So, we cannot take the risk of eliminating him. That would be disastrous.'

Dilawar Khan said, 'But Boss, if I may ask…what exactly is his problem?'

Bakhtawar sighed and said, 'He belongs to a new era of politics, in which people think about the growth and development of the country. He is a highly educated person. He is qualified from London and dreams of bringing Utopia to Pakistan. He believes that everyone should live in peace and happiness. He wants to see Pakistan become a prosperous country. He wants to empower the common man of Pakistan. He wants to eliminate all the terrorist camps in Pakistan… That is where our problem starts.'

Dilawar Khan thought for a while. In his mind, he agreed with Khwaja Salahudeen. Why should the people suffer for no fault of theirs? Why should there be more and more Dilawar Khans breeding from Pakistani soil because of a heavily lopsided social structure? But he did not dare utter these thoughts in front of the Boss for obvious reasons.

Instead he said thoughtfully, 'So…our plan is to…'

Bakhtawar said, 'As I said before, we don't want to harm him. We just want to teach him a lesson. I have decided that we will kidnap his daughter studying in high school and ask for a ransom. He will definitely give us the money as we assume that he has a lot of money, but I want him to experience a few tense hours when we tell him that his daughter is in our custody and that she will be set free only after he meets our conditions. We expect that this will make him realise that he would be playing with fire if he still goes out after us.'

Dilawar Khan said, 'Yes Boss. Agree with you. So, what is the next move?'

'Start planning, as usual,' Bakhtawar said. 'Study the details about his daughter. Find out where she goes, where she studies, does she go out regularly anywhere after the school etc. Please come to me with a proper plan after two weeks.'

Dilawar Khan nodded his head, engrossed in deep thought, and left the meeting place. He had a lot of work to do now. With some preliminary enquiries, he found out that every member of Khwaja Salahudeen's family was provided with tight security due to the changed circumstances in Pakistan. The life of the common man had become extremely risky and anything could happen anytime in Pakistan. There were several terror groups working in isolation and they all had different objectives and targets. But the heat was faced by the common man, who found it very difficult to move around safely. There were bomb explosions every other day, killing scores of people. The rich and famous had already bought security for themselves through armed guards from private companies. The senior Government officials used their influence with the police department to get a guard or two for themselves. The Home Minister was a sensitive target and hence there was a high degree of protection for him and his family members.

Over the next few days, Dilawar Khan found out that Khwaja Slahudeen's daughter's name was Maliha and she was studying in Grade 10 of a reputed high school called New Model High School. She went to school in a car with red beacon lights flashing, followed by a police jeep. It was impossible to try anything while she was going to the school or returning, as there was armed security protecting her. She did not go out anywhere after school; two tuition teachers visited her house in the evening.

The school had two security guards posted outside the main gate, so any attempt to do anything near the school was also difficult. Dilawar Khan was clueless as to how he was going to kidnap her. He was a trusted and trained resource of the Organisation and he needed to find a way to attain the objective. He started thinking of a way to enter the school. He was not sure what he would do by entering the school, since any attempt to kidnap her from there would be disastrous, as the gates were guarded and the Home Minister's security vehicle outside would intercept him immediately, if ever such an attempt was made.

After almost one week of brainstorming, he came up with an idea. What if he entered the school as a courier boy? Nobody would suspect him. That would also give him an opportunity to go inside the school premises and get a broad idea of the school layout, at least from the main entrance till the administrative office. So, he went to the market and bought the latest copy of the weekly magazine, 'Weekly Pulse'. He then went to a typing institute and typed the address of the school with 'To, The Head Master' at the top of the address slip. He put the magazine in an envelope and pasted the address slip. He then wrote a random 10-digit number on the envelope on the top left side as if it was a courier registration number. He was now ready to enter the school premises.

The next day, he went to the school in the garb of a courier delivery person and told the security that he had a courier to be delivered. He was an expert in disguise, so for this occasion, he had disguised himself perfectly. He wore a wig of slightly overgrown hair, a thin beard and a small moustache. The security guard looked at him for a moment and then allowed him to go inside, guiding him to the office. He walked to the office appearing very casual but he was noting each and every minute detail inside the school premises. He observed that the compound wall was around 8-feet high. He walked through the ground, and reached a corridor at the end of which was the office. He handed over the envelope in the office. No one in the office would ever know whether the Head Master had ordered the magazine or the publisher had sent a complimentary copy to the school. He promptly took the acknowledgement sheet with the signature of the office clerk and started walking back to the gate. While passing through the corridor, he glanced at the various paintings made by the students, which were displayed on the corridor walls on both sides. He wondered at the amazing skill and creativity displayed by such young students in art.

Suddenly his attention was grabbed by a notice board with some notices. He looked further and observed one notice which read, 'Required Physical Instructor for High School'. He went closer to the notice board and learnt that the school was inviting applications for the position of a Physical Instructor for the high school students. In a flash of inspiration he thought, how about joining the school as a Physical Instructor? Then he would have access to the entire school premises and no one would suspect him of any foul play. He would also get the time to think and find out more details about Maliha which would probably give him more ideas on how to proceed further in his mission. As a general rule, he believed that when faced with a big task, it is advisable to break the task down into smaller fragments. Then take one step after another step. His logic was that when you stand on the ground, you can see up to a certain distance. When you stand on a table, you can see a little farther. And when you stand on the terrace, you can see still farther. So, one should not just stand on the ground and make plans with inadequate data.

Within the next three days, the Boss arranged some false certificates for him with a dummy name. With these certificates, Dilawar Khan applied for the vacant position of Physical Instructor in the school. After a week he was called for the interview. Since he was well trained in various physical activities in the Organisation's academy, his physique was in pretty good shape. He was instantly selected as the physical instructor for high school classes. He had a different identity in the school now. It was very easy to get a fake degree or diploma in any subject in Pakistan. One of his friends had a hobby collecting several degrees and diplomas and had collected 23 such certificates.

Dilawar Khan joined the school the next week and went about his tasks calmly. He did not want to appear suspicious in any manner to either the students or the other teachers in the school. Within three days he learnt from a peon in the school that Khwaja Salahudeen's daughter was studying in section C of grade 10. He had six classes for physical activity every day, for various sections and 10C was on every Wednesday afternoon. He eagerly waited for Wednesday afternoon to meet his next prey.

On Wednesday afternoon, the class of 10C began. He introduced himself to all the students. He told them that physical activity was very important for everyone as it helps them to keep fit and be in the best of health. A healthy lifestyle was a must for a person to experience happiness in life. Saying so, he asked all the students to introduce themselves. And in the third row, a bright student said, 'I am Maliha…' Dilawar Khan carefully looked at her. He had found her…finally. She appeared to be one of those brilliant students who were good at everything they do. They are good at studies of course, but apart from that they are also good in other areas like sports, quiz competitions, art, dance and music etc. From that day onwards, he started giving her special attention. She too liked the attention.

Once Dilawar Khan started going to the school as a Physical Instructor, he started enjoying the atmosphere within the school. This was probably the first time that he was seeing any school at such close quarters and in a positive light. He was very happy to see the small children of all ages come every morning to school, dressed up neatly in their school uniforms, carrying school bags and tiffin baskets. He loved to see them sitting in groups during lunch time, sharing their food with one another. He was seeing life in its purest form there.

He remembered his school days. They were totally different from what he was seeing here. He had studied in an ordinary Government school which was not so well managed. The teachers were not interested in developing the children and the building, classrooms etc were not so great. It was more or less like the children were dumped there by their parents to fend for themselves. The children needed to make all the efforts to study and learn. It was a logical conclusion therefore, as to what kind of students the school produced. All his classmates were very average in their studies and no one went on to occupy any respectable positions in society.

And he realised for the first time, the importance of an education system in any country's development. If any country had any plans for good progress and development, all it needed to do was to provide healthy and positive education system for the primary and secondary school system. Those were the years when children learnt the basics of various subjects. They learnt basic etiquette and moral values of society. They learnt how to read, write and talk. At that age, children are highly flexible and can easily mould themselves into whichever way they are shaped.

It was a Government's obligatory duty to ensure that all children in the country are put through a sound education system. These children are the citizens of tomorrow. He speculated how in the next twenty years, some of these children would be engineers, doctors, lawyers and scientists etc. And in another twenty years, they would probably be managing important positions in society like owning private companies or heading Government departments etc. It seemed funny that these children were going to grow up and become responsible. He was rather remorseful that he had grown to become a terrorist. While he did not like to call himself a terrorist, he knew that the work he did was that of a terrorist only. He had never thought of marriage, but for the first time he wondered, if he ever got married and had children, what would he tell them about his profession? Would he tell them the truth or a lie? And if at all he said the truth, would he say that with a feeling of remorse or a sense of pride? He had no answer to these questions as of now.

He wanted his children to look up at him with respect and reverence. Would they do so if he ever told them his real profession? It was doubtful. In fact, he did not respect his father much because he did not provide him suitable basic education during his formative years. But now, he realised that at least his father had been an honest person who never harmed anyone. He had just toiled throughout the day in order to feed his large family. In that sense, his father was a far superior person in comparison to Dilawar, purely going by the way he had chosen to live his life so far. Life is nothing but a series of decisions made by an individual. At every stage, life offers everyone some options or alternatives. Life and destiny is shaped based on what route the person takes. Sometimes, life also puts a person in a situation where the options are limited and no favourable route seems available ahead. At such times the real grit of the person is brought to the fore.

Dilawar Khan soon became a favourite teacher for many students of his class. He would inspire them to perform better and better in their games and activities. His striking physique also made him appealing to many students. People around him noticed his good behaviour and they started actually liking him. He used to interact with Maliha as well, whenever he was taking their class. Maliha would look at him with respect. On many occasions he had inspired her to improve her skills in games by giving her the right tips and guidance. While training her on various sports, he instilled in her values of competitive sports and the qualities of sportsmanship. He advised her that at times, when playing in a team, she might be required to help others as well, for the team to win. A brilliant individual performance is of no use if the team loses. He also taught her that failure in sports is to be taken as a lesson and used as positive feedback to improve one's performance in the future. In sports, one cannot expect to win every time and someone has to lose in every game.

Over the next few days, Dilawar Khan became friends with some other teachers of the school as well. In fact, he started loving the school environment. He was enjoying the school atmosphere, as it fostered a hope, for a better tomorrow. He felt that all the educational institutes around the world are temples of the civilisation and modern society. If the world is what it is today, it was because of these places and if the world needed to get better, these places had the biggest responsibility of achieving that goal. He also felt that every government should make education mandatory for all children up to secondary level at least. That would give every child in this world an opportunity to know about the world, about the history of the world and he would then be in a better position to decide what is good and what is bad for him. Without this minimum education, a child may never be aware of the vast possibilities existing in this world and his hidden potential to achieve anything in his life. He felt pity for the children of underdeveloped countries around the world who did not have basic education and were struggling all through their life to make both ends meet. Was it possible that if they had been given a proper education, some of them would have excelled in any field and achieved more success than what has been achieved by successful people today in those fields? So, was it not the 'Opportunity Cost' paid by society for not educating these children? And who is answerable for this intangible loss to the world and mankind? Was it the Government of these underdeveloped countries? Or was it the people who elected those Governments? It was a difficult question.

Once, Dilawar Khan also happened to pass in front of the school library. He was curious about the books and magazines kept there. So he went inside and looked at the neatly stacked books inside numerous shelves there. He was amazed to see the number of books available on various subjects. He was awed at the sight of so many books. He wondered whether it was physically possible for anyone to read all those books. How much time would be required to read all these books? For the first time he realised that one life was too short to learn all the knowledge available in the world. It all depended on the individual and how he chose to spend his time in life. If he consciously chose to learn more things, he automatically became wiser, and whoever chose not to learn new things remained ignorant. For time is limited and granted equally to all individuals.

The priorities chosen by the people defined their future. For the first time he also felt sad at not being properly educated during his time in school. He wondered whether this was an opportunity given by the Almighty for him to continue his learning.

However, all his fanciful thoughts and intellectual dreaming were brought to an abrupt halt when he received a call from Bakhtawar one evening.

'Dilawar, how are things? Any progress made?

Dilawar Khan was not expecting his call. He blurted out, 'Sorry Boss, things are fine here. Progress for...?

He had momentarily forgotten that he had been sent to this school on a mission: to kidnap Khwaja Salahudeen's daughter Maliha, studying in 10th grade.

Before Bakhtawar could react, Dilawar Khan continued, 'Oh yes. Yes, I am planning to execute the kidnapping soon. I am getting used to the school layout now. The problem is that all the school entrance and exit gates are guarded during school hours. And as you are aware, she commutes to school in an escorted vehicle.'

Bakhtawar sensed that Dilawar Khan was in some way not displaying urgency in the matter. He said, 'So what do you plan to do? Wait for the summer...or winter?'

Dilawar Khan realized that Bakhtawar was slightly angry. He said, 'No Boss, please try to understand. I am trying my best to make a plan. Inshallah, soon I shall let you know about my plan and also the scheduled dates for implementation.

Bakhtawar said curtly, 'You better get on with your real job soon. We do not want to waste time on useless things.' And he hung up.

Dilawar Khan was lost in thoughts. He had an urge to ask the Boss, whether it was necessary to kidnap the girl? He had developed a soft corner for all the students in the school. He felt that the entire world's innocence, love and purity of thoughts were reflected in each and every child's face in the school. The nation was being gradually formed each day, each minute in that school and all other schools around the world. He wanted to contribute to the process of nation building. He had not done anything positive in his life till date that could have made him or his family proud. Now was the time when he felt he should repay the moral debt of being a true Pakistani. He wanted to be a part of the system which converted small sublime minds into great intellectuals shaping the policies of Pakistan. Once he kidnapped Maliha, his association with the school would come to an end and he would possibly never ever step into the same school again. He did not want to be away from this immensely positively charged environment where every morning, the little children walked into the school with little dreams in their eyes.

The next day, in the library, he found a little book called 'Essence of Quran'. He picked it up and read it during his free period. And he learnt so many new things about his religion, which he had never known before. He realised that Islam actually preached peace and harmony among all the people. There was no mention about harming anyone in any section of the Holy Quran. He wondered why the trainers in his Organisation's camp spewed venom every day while preaching to the new recruits and trainees. They only spoke in a language of hatred and revenge. For the first time, he felt cheated. He could not imagine why the so-called preachers did not profess peace and love, as mentioned in the Holy Quran?

He sincerely thought that he would execute this kidnapping mission as his last and final assignment and then think of parting ways with the Organisation. He had spent his early life in poverty and misery. Ever since he started taking his own decisions, he had lived the life of a rogue, a terrorist, who killed people mercilessly. However, the last few days in this school had almost transformed him. He was strongly reminded of jailor Yashwant's lessons which had taught him the positive aspects of life. He had not paid much attention to those moral lessons then, but now, in hindsight he felt that those lessons were very valuable. Whatever he remembered about Yashwant's teachings now seemed very good from his revised perspective of life.

He decided firmly in his mind that once the kidnapping episode was over, and the ransom paid, he would mend his ways. He actively started looking for a suitable opportunity.

Soon Dilawar Khan spotted the moment he was waiting for. The school had organised a trekking trip for 8th, 9th and 10th grade students next month. They planned to take these students to Margalla Hills National Park near Islamabad for mountaineering. As the Physical Instructor for high school, he was of course required to go with the students. An academy was hired to provide all the logistic support like ropes, hooks, and special safety equipment etc. Two trainers from the academy would also assist the students. Dilawar Khan knew that this was the best opportunity to execute his plan.

That evening, he took out a map of Margalla Hills National Park. He carefully studied all the entry and exit points. He realised that once they were into the mountains, there were several routes from which they could escape. However, he needed to ensure that he kidnapped her without any onlooker getting suspicious. Otherwise the whole plan would flop and he would end up in a soup.

He spoke to the Boss about the impending trip and his plan to implement the kidnapping then. The Boss was happy to know that the opportunity was coming soon, when he could teach the Home Minister a lesson to mind his own business and leave the Organisation alone. He had further discussions with Dilawar Khan on the smaller details and hung up. He advised Dilawar Khan to call him after three days to know where the girl would be held in captivity during the kidnapped period.

The following week, the Boss and Dilawar Khan made a complete plan of the kidnapping. According to the plan, Dilawar Khan would guide Maliha to a slightly different route while trekking and then get down from a different route, where a car would be waiting for them to be taken to a guest house, located around 40 km from the Park. Once Dilawar Khan took the girl to the guest house, Bakhtawar would call the Home Minister and ask for the ransom. They anticipated that they would have to keep the girl in the captivity for a period of 2-3 days, which was the expected time for negotiating the deal on the terms and conditions of the ransom. The guest house was equipped with enough food to sustain them for three days. They wanted to avoid any movement around the guest house once they were in, to avoid attracting the attention of the neighbours, even though they were a bit far off.

As the day approached, Dilawar Khan was feeling nostalgic. He wished he could be in this school forever. He did not want to leave the pure atmosphere of the school where every day, young minds were being shaped incrementally by dedicated teachers. He was inspired by just looking at the innocence all around him. He felt happy to see the unadulterated happiness flowing around him in the young children. Once he kidnapped Maliha, he would never ever come back to the school again. He had heard somewhere that duty should always take precedence over the emotions of a person. Unfortunately, currently, his duties were demanding actions that contradicted with his emotions. However, a duty was a duty and it always needed to be honoured.

Finally the day arrived for the trekking expedition. Dilawar Khan had carefully eliminated all identification clues from his rented house near the school, as he knew that by the same evening, the police would be searching for him like hungry wolves. He went to the school with a rucksack containing all his essential items. At 8am, three buses started from the school to Margalla National Park. Dilawar Khan noticed that a police jeep was also escorting them as a precautionary measure. He confirmed that Maliha was also present in one of the buses. He was looking out of the window thinking deeply about his action plan. He had not yet thought about how he was going to get Maliha to the car without any resistance. He had to be extremely careful in doing that because any visible display of force by him or resistance by her would alert the people around him immediately and his plan would fail. Over the last few weeks, ever since Dilawar Khan had joined the school, he had developed some kind of respect for Maliha. She was a brilliant girl who was very well mannered too. She was charming and displayed no attitude while playing with other children in spite of her father being a VIP. He felt that she had all the qualities of a dream child for any parents. And that made his task somewhat more difficult. His genuine respect for her made him worry whether he would be able to carry out his task well or falter at the last minute.

The moment the children got down from the buses, there was excitement all around. The children were all geared up for the day that promised adventures and thrills. The teachers bought the entrance tickets and lined up all the students to take them inside. Once they went in, they were divided into groups to be managed by the respective teachers for better control over all of them. By sheer coincidence, Dilawar Khan was in charge of the group which had Maliha in it. He was happy. His task was now going to be slightly easier.

He led the group of children to the designated trekking point. He knew that beyond a peak visible to him, a car would be waiting for them. He cheered all the children to start climbing uphill. He ensured that everyone had proper protection with them. There were eight children in his group. He was moving close to Maliha. He did not want to miss this opportunity which the Boss had been waiting for, for over a few months now.

When they had reached almost over half the distance, Dilawar Khan turned to Maliha and said, 'Come on Maliha, you need to be first.'

She looked at him, smiled and started going ahead of the group faster than before. She was motivated to reach the top faster. She was enthused at the prospect of standing at the top of a small hillock in the backdrop of bigger mountains. She reached the top and started looking beyond. Dilawar Khan reached as well and stood behind her. His mind was racing now as to how to enact his plan. The other girls were still climbing and needed to cover some distance to reach to the point where they were standing now.

The moment had arrived…

Dilawar Khan suddenly turned towards Maliha and said, 'Maliha, come fast.' He caught her hand and started dragging her down the other side of the slope along with him. For a moment she did not understand what was happening. Since they were climbing down the slope, their attention was focussed on watching their steps, so that they wouldn't trip and fall. Descending a mountain slope is much more difficult than climbing it, as there is every chance of slipping. However, she kept on half-walking and half-running with him trying to figure out what was happening.

Soon, they saw an old white car ready there waiting for them. The car had dark, tinted glasses so that no one from outside could see who was sitting inside the car. He opened the back door and pushed her into the car and sat beside her. He ordered the driver to start the car. By now, Maliha was a bit scared, wondering what was happening. She had never doubted Dilawar Khan before. She had always appreciated his toned body and felt that he was a gentleman who exercised a lot to keep his body in good shape. She appreciated his agile movements on the school ground while running or during other sporting activities.

Therefore, she did not panic per se, but was definitely worried about what was happening. Everything had happened in three to four minutes from the time he took her from the top of the hillock to the car. She asked Dilawar Khan, 'Sir, what is happening? Where are we going?'

Dilawar Khan looked at her with assurance in his eyes and said, 'See Maliha, we are playing a reality show here. Don't worry, everything is alright.'

Maliha was further surprised at this statement. She looked questioningly at Dilawar Khan and asked, 'Sir, what do you mean reality show? Where are we going?'

Dilawar Khan said calmly, 'Look Maliha, your father is Home Minister, right? He just wanted to check how alert the security system in Pakistan is. He wanted to see how fast they can track us down and find out where we are hiding.'

Maliha was not convinced. She said disbelievingly, 'But my Abba did not say anything about this to me. He would have definitely told me before of his plan.'

Dilawar Khan said, 'See, he wanted this plan to be top secret. He felt that you might talk about this plan to the school authorities or to the police personnel accompanying us on this expedition. Therefore, he took only me into confidence so that the plan remains top secret.'

Maliha was still not convinced. She questioned, 'But how do you know my Abba? When did he talk to you? Where are we going to hide? I need to talk to my Abba now...'

Dilawar Khan said, 'See Maliha, your Abba is a very honest politician. He wanted to see how safe an ordinary citizen of Pakistan is today. And for that purpose only has he decided to play this reality show to check the efficiency of the system.'

Maliha did not know what to say. Her heart was asking her to believe Dilawar Khan, but her mind was warning her of danger. She said, 'Where are we going now?'

'Just an hour's drive from here. We shall be staying in a guest house till they can find us. Then you can go home. As simple as that...'

Maliha was a bit relieved when the mention of her going home came into his discussion. She did not say anything. She just kept looking out of the car window at the beauty of nature outside.

They reached the guest house in an hour. There were three people with rifles surrounding it. Maliha thought that they were the security guards meant to protect her. However, she did notice that they were not in uniform, which made her somewhat suspicious.

Dilawar Khan switched on the TV set to watch the local news channel. Breaking News was flashing, 'Home Minister's daughter missing.' The TV reporters were standing in the Margalla National Park reporting that the girl had come here on an expedition that day and was not seen after climbing a small hillock. Several search teams were combing the park in all the directions.

By now Maliha was getting slightly disturbed. She desperately wanted to know the truth. Why did her Abba think of making such a plan without informing her? Did he not bother to think how worried she would be while the plan was being enacted? She looked at Dilawar Khan, who was closely watching the news with no expression on his face.

He offered her some fruits and biscuits. He said, 'See Maliha, there is no need to worry. You are very safe here. Your safety is my concern.' She started eating as she suddenly realised that she was very hungry.

While she was wondering what to do next, suddenly she thought that she could call her Abba and find out the truth. She asked Dilawar Khan, 'Sir, I want to talk to my Abba.'

Dilawar Khan said, 'No, you can't.'

She was taken aback. Her suspicion was increasing. And then some more Breaking News flashed on the TV screen, 'Maliha and the Physical Instructor of the school are missing.'

The TV cameras showed Maliha's mother sobbing and saying, 'Where is my Maliha? How is she? I want her back…'

Seeing this, Maliha instantly felt tears in her eyes. She stood up and told Dilawar Khan, 'I want to talk to my mother. I can't see her crying like this for me.'

Dilawar Khan was unmoved. He said, 'Sorry Maliha, there is no landline connection here and I will not allow you to call your parents from my mobile.'

It was then that Maliha realised that there was definitely something wrong. She looked fearfully at Dilawar Khan and asked, 'Sir, Who are you? And why are you doing this to me?'

Dilawar Khan thought for a while and said, 'Maliha, I am a terrorist and I have kidnapped you. My Boss will be contacting your Abba soon to ask for ransom money. Once it is paid, you will be released. Believe me, we will not harm you, as long as you and your Abba cooperate with us…'

Maliha felt as if the ground was slipping from under her feet. She felt that she was too young to face this kind of a situation. But then, emergencies in life do not look at age, religion or caste…they just come like unexpected guests. That is why they are called emergencies.

She could hear her heart beating loudly. Her legs had a slight shiver. Her mouth was going dry. Dilawar Khan sensed her condition and helped her to sit on the sofa. She just closed her eyes and rested her head on the back of the seat. Her mind was going numb. She was in a terrible situation. A really terrible situation! She had heard about such incidents in the past, but had never faced them.

And in the next few minutes, the Breaking News changed to, 'It is suspected that the Physical Instructor of the School has kidnapped Maliha…'

That night Dilawar Khan had dinner with Maliha and advised her to sleep in a separate bedroom. He advised her not to make any foolish attempts to escape from the guest house, as it was guarded round the clock. By now, she had gained some amount of confidence that Dilawar Khan would at least not harm her. If he had any such plans, he would have done so by now. All the while he had said that she was safe, so she thought of believing him on that front. Anyway, he had confessed to her that she had been kidnapped and would be safely returned to her family after the agreed ransom amount was paid.

In the morning, Maliha got up as usual and wondered how she could have slept in captivity at all. But then, when the body is tired and mind is stressed, sleep would automatically come.

At the breakfast table, she asked Dilawar Khan, 'Sir, why did you kidnap only me? And what are you asking for as ransom?'

Dilawar Khan first thought he would not answer her. But then somewhere in his mind he respected her.

Whether it was respect for her knowledge, or her attitude, or her manner, he did not know. He slowly explained, 'See Maliha, your Abba is not a good person. He wants to develop Pakistan by eliminating terrorists. We want to teach him a lesson to mind his own business.'

Maliha said, 'Sir, but he is minding his own business. As a Home Minister, his foremost duty is to ensure the safety and security of all the citizens of Pakistan. If he is taking steps to achieve that goal, how can he be wrong?'

Dilawar Khan was surprised at her courage to put forward such a logical statement, the maturity of which was not commensurate with her age. He said, 'Yes, but we too have to live, right? Where do we go if Pakistan is all cleaned up?'

Maliha said, 'Sir, you are not nationals of any country. Once you are fighting your battle against your own country, you are not its citizens any more. You are traitors.' She looked at him wondering whether she had spoken more than she should have. But he did not appear to take any offence at her statement.

He said, 'Maliha, you do not know how many risks we take in our daily lives. The life of a terrorist is not an easy one...'

Maliha said, 'Sir, agreed. But who asked you to become a terrorist? You are not respected by anyone in society. The police and the army are always behind you. You have respect and recognition within your Organisation only, nowhere else.'

For the first time, someone had raised questions on why he had become a terrorist.

She continued, 'If you take risks in living an immoral life, it is not honourable at all. On the contrary, if you lead an ordinary simple life within the system, by complying with its rules and regulations, it is far more honourable.'

Dilawar Khan thought for a while. He remembered his early days when he had been in bad company. He had never received a proper education or moral support from his family. He wondered, if he had received good education what would he have become. In such a scenario, he would have been in a much better position to argue intellectually with Maliha. However, if he had studied well, he may not have become a terrorist in the first place.

He said, 'Look Maliha, I am in no mood to discuss this with you or convince you about why I am the way I am. I am the way I am…that's it. We cannot change the past. Right?'

She said, 'True sir, you need not convince me about why you are the way you are. But you also said that you cannot change the past. Does it mean that if given a chance you would opt for a different past?'

The question struck him straight in his heart. Yes, definitely he would opt for a different past, if he was offered an option by the Almighty. Which terrorist would have had a happy and joyous childhood? Practically none! Every terrorist must have had a very troublesome and grievous childhood. Otherwise who would really enjoy going on a rampage killing innocent people for no fault of theirs? What fun could anyone have by causing harm to unsuspecting fellow human beings? It was definitely not a sane person's job.

Dilawar Khan replied to the question half heartedly, 'See Maliha, as I said before, we cannot change the past. So the question is purely hypothetical and I am not interested in answering hypothetical questions.'

Maliha said firmly, 'Sir, agreed. You cannot change your past. But by changing now, you can surely change your future. Today you are based on what you did yesterday. Tomorrow you will be based on what you do today.'

This moral lecture was becoming too much for Dilawar Khan. He left the room and looked out of the window from another room. He suddenly remembered Yashwant. He used to give similar moral lectures to Dilawar Khan in the fond hope that he would really change one day. Somehow he felt that Maliha's moral preaching was evoking a similar effect in his mind.

Chapter 9

The TV news was now showing speculative theories on how Dilawar Khan would have kidnapped Maliha. By now, the TV reporters had also gone to Dilawar Khan's residence address as recorded in the school records and found out that he had left no clues about his whereabouts. The investigating agencies realised that the entire documentation provided by Dilawar Khan during his appointment as Physical Instructor in the school was fake and as a result, gave them no clue about his whereabouts or contacts.

And then the call came to the Home Minister, Khwaja Salahudeen from an unknown mobile number. The caller was Bakhtawar. He said, 'How are you Home Minister Sahaab?'

Khwaja Salahudeen said, 'I am fine. Who is this?' He hoped that the call was from someone with some information about his daughter.

Bakhtawar said, 'Don't worry about who I am. Please know that your daughter is in our custody and she is safe. Nothing will happen to her if you follow our instructions.'

Khwaja Salahudeen was suddenly relieved and also worried at the mention of his daughter after so many hours. He said, 'Yes...yes. Please tell me what I have to do. I want my daughter back safely at any cost.'

Bakhtawar said, 'Well, I knew that you would pay any price to get your daughter back. But first, listen carefully. No police or army to be involved. We hate those people.'

Khwaja Salahudeen replied hastily, 'Ok…ok.'

Bakhtawar said, 'I want rupees ten crores as ransom.'

'See, I am not a rich politician,' Khwaja Salahudeen protested. 'I do not have that much money to pay.'

Bakhtawar raised his voice, 'If you are not rich, that is not my problem, Mr. Khwaja Salahudeen. Moreover, if you don't want to make money in politics, why are you in politics? Go and open a school for yourself in Rawalpindi.'

Salahudeen listened helplessly.

Bakhtawar continued, 'And yes. We also want you to release 10 of our members arrested by the police and army in the last six months. We shall send you the names by tomorrow.'

Salahudeen said, 'See whoever you are, this is not the right thing that you are doing. Please do not harm my daughter. We love her very much…'

Bakhtawar said, 'Good. Start gathering the money. I shall call you in the evening. And yes, don't try to trace my call. You will reach nowhere. I use a different SIM card every time and throw it away after calling once.'

Salahudeen said, 'See, I beg you …' but realised that the caller had hung up.

Salahudeen dropped onto the sofa as his legs gave way. His wife, Razia, who had been listening to his side of the conversation, came near him and asked him what the kidnappers had asked.

Salahudeen said, 'They are asking us for rupees ten crores. And they also want us to release ten hardcore terrorists captured by the Government.'

Razia was already in a state of depression ever since Maliha had been kidnapped. She got even more upset on hearing the demands of the kidnappers. She knew that they did not have that kind of money to pay the ransom. She also knew that it was against Salahudeen's principles to release hardcore terrorists caught by the brave acts of policemen and army personnel. So, both the demands of the kidnappers appeared to be too difficult to meet.

Salahudeen thought for a while and called the police control room. After all, he was in charge of the entire police department of Pakistan. If he did not believe in their capabilities and seek their help, how could he expect the common man to feel confident about them? Razia was afraid that her husband's call to the police department would be detrimental to their daughter's safety. She did not know what to pray for. On one side was her husband who was a righteous, patriotic person for whom duty came above emotion, and on the other side was her emotional heart, the heart of a mother, which refused to acknowledge logic and rationale at a difficult time like this.

Salahudeen asked the police commissioner to trace the call, knowing that they would not be able to really get anywhere.

But, as they say, hope is life.

Dilawar Khan offered his prayers and came to the living room where Maliha was watching the news on TV. The investigating agencies had not made much headway in tracing where the kidnappers had kept Maliha in captivity. However, different teams were working fulltime to gather clues about the whereabouts of Dilawar Khan and Maliha.

While they both were watching the news, Breaking News appeared that the kidnappers had demanded a ransom of rupees ten crores and also asking for the release of 10 hardcore terrorists captured by the police during the last six months.

Maliha looked at Dilawar Khan and said, 'How mean can you people get, sir? My Abba does not have that amount of money. And what is this condition of releasing 10 terrorists? I am sure my Abba would not agree to that condition at least.'

Dilawar Khan was surprised. Here was a young girl in captivity, forecasting that her father would not fulfil the conditions set forth by the kidnappers for her safe release.

He said, 'Do you mean to say that your Abba would not comply with our demands?'

Maliha said, 'Yes sir. I am sure he is a person of principles who believes in protecting the honour and dignity of his office. He may agree to pay the ransom amount by borrowing it from somewhere, but he would never agree to release the terrorists from jail.'

Dilawar Khan was even more surprised at this explanation. He said, 'Are you saying that he would not mind losing you, just to protect his so called honour and dignity of office? And may I know, what makes you think so?'

Maliha said, 'Sir, I know my Abba very well. He is on a mission to clean up Pakistan. He is not like other politicians of today, who are in politics only to amass huge wealth and live a luxurious life by misusing the powers associated with their position in the Government. My Abba wants to see a good Pakistan which is free from corruption, which is advanced in technology, which cares for its citizens and provides them adequate safety.'

Dilawar Khan was amazed at the knowledge of this young high school girl. For the first time he acknowledged in his mind that her Abba was doing a good job; he had at least made his daughter aware of the current situation in Pakistan and his dreams. He had taught her what good values meant.

Dilawar Khan said, 'And how is he going to achieve these tasks? Is he aware of the difficulties involved in even attempting to achieve these goals?

Maliha replied, 'Yes sir. He is a true Muslim who believes in the powers of Allah and follows the path as shown in the Holy Quran. Anyone who has faith and belief in the Quran, who practices the advice given in the Quran, can surmount any challenges in this world. I am confident about that.'

Dilawar Khan said, 'Sorry Maliha, just by following religion, a country cannot move forward. Even we follow Islam. We read prayers regularly. Everyone in Pakistan prays very religiously. Why is the country not progressing in spite of all these prayers?'

'Sir, I am sorry to say that you are not following Islam in a true fashion,' Said Maliha. 'You are actually spoiling the name of Islam around the world. It is people like you who indulge in acts which are not prescribed in any religious scriptures of Islam and the whole community has to face the brunt of it.'

Now Dilawar Khan was becoming angry but thoughtful as well. He said, 'Do you know the atrocities taking place regularly against our brothers in some other countries? Do you know the sufferings of Muslims in those places? Are we not supposed to protect them? Are we not supposed to fight for their cause? Is it not our religious duty?'

Maliha said, 'Yes sir. I agree that there could be some problems in other countries against Muslims. But don't you think that you are looking at only one side of the story? Moreover, have you ever considered that any issue can always be resolved through dialogue and discussion? Just because someone suffers somewhere, it does not give you the right to interfere and create violence there.'

Dilawar Khan was forced to think about what Maliha said, as it seemed quite logical. He had never thought about this before. He had been totally brainwashed at the training camps when he was inducted into the Organisation, that they were on a Holy Mission and that their actions would be considered righteous on the Day of Judgment. This was the first time someone had challenged his ideas and beliefs.

He returned to the original topic and said, 'So you are saying that your Abba will not release our 10 colleagues from jail?'

Maliha said, 'Yes sir. Imagine how many risks those policemen would have taken in capturing these terrorists? Do you want it to go to waste? Imagine how many people these terrorists might have killed so far? Do you want that they should go unpunished for that offence? A criminal must face punishment to restore the faith of the common man in the judiciary and the laws of the land. Otherwise the citizens of this country will stop believing in the entire system of governance, the law and order, and the process of the judiciary.'

Dilawar Khan realised that Maliha was very firm in her opinion about her Abba. He wondered whether Khwaja Salahudeen would really not agree to the conditions set by the Organisation for Maliha's release. He left the room and started thinking deeply.

The tension was palpable in Khwaja Salahudeen's house. He was at a loss on the way forward. He had his ideals, dreams and ambitions on one side and his lovely daughter on the other side. The way things were moving, he could not have them both together. He had to sacrifice one to save the other. Razia was looking at him helplessly, hoping that he would opt for his daughter's safe release. She was equally respectful of his ideology and his objectives but being a mother, her heart was having a say over her mind and logic. They were anxiously waiting for the next call from the kidnappers to negotiate the ransom amount and other conditions.

Bakhtawar called the Home Minister again in the evening and said in an irritated tone, 'So, in spite of my warning you sought help from the police, right?'

Salahudeen said helplessly, 'Yes. I am in-charge of the security of every citizen in this country and if I do not have trust and faith in them, how can anyone else believe in them?'

Bakhtawar was angry. He said, 'So, just to prove that your security system is trustworthy, you are ready to risk your daughter's life?'

Salahudeen said, 'I plead with you to release my daughter. Please do not harm her…'

Bakhtawar said, 'Salahudeen Sahaab, I am equally confident that your security system can never catch me. Anyway, you are limiting your options with your actions. By the way, what have you decided about my demands? Shall I tell you the names of people to be released? Is the money arranged?'

Salahudeen took a deep breath and said, 'Look, whoever you are, I am not a rich person to offer you that kind of money. I need time to collect such a big amount. As regards releasing the terrorists from the prisons, I do not agree. The brave people of our security system risked their lives while capturing these terrorists. We do not want their efforts to go waste. Otherwise, no policeman in Pakistan will ever show any enthusiasm in catching criminals. They will lose faith in the political system, which would be very bad for the country's progress. Please ask for something else.'

Bakhtawar was surprised at this straight denial of his demands by Salahudeen. He said, 'Salahudeen Sahaab, I am surprised. You are ready to lose your precious daughter for protecting your ideals and values? What can you alone do Mr. Salahudeen? You are living in a fool's paradise if you believe that you can singlehandedly bring about a change in the system, which is currently filled to the brim with selfish and corrupt people who have no regard whatsoever for the well being of this country.'

Salahudeen said, 'See, every major revolution starts with one person. It takes just one person to initiate a movement. One person with a dream in his eyes and passion for achieving his goal can make the masses move. I do not mind if I have to even sacrifice my beloved daughter in this process of cleaning up the system.'

Bakhtawar said, 'Now I am truly surprised, Salahudeen Sahaab. You seem to be a man in a hurry to clean up the system. And that is where our problem starts. Why don't you mind your own business and allow us to do our work peacefully?'

'No way,' said Salahudeen. 'My job is only to control and eliminate the activities of people like you who are working against the nation. And I shall pray to Allah to give me the strength to ensure that my legs do not shake when I am going about my job. I pray to him to grant me courage when the goal appears slightly distant or there are temporary setbacks in my mission. I want him to keep me inspired to continue in my efforts.'

Bakhtawar wondered what he would do to Maliha in case the demands were not met. As per the basic rules of the Organisation, in a kidnapping case, if the demands were not met, or if police help was sought by defying the Organisation's warning, the only consequence was to kill the kidnapped person. There was no second thought about it. If they started showing leniency in such cases, tomorrow no one would even care for them. Their fear factor would go down gradually and they would be out of business.

Bakhtawar did not want to end the negotiation process just yet. He said, 'Dear Home Minister, I am so sorry to hear all that spirited talk from you. Did you think that you were giving an election speech and that I was a voter standing in front of you, listening to you? Sorry, by being adamant about your views, you are gradually reducing our options about how we deal with you. I shall give you time till tomorrow morning. And remember, I shall not call again thereafter. Please think well and make up your mind by then. Finally, let me also warn you that if the talks fail tomorrow morning, be assured that you may never see your daughter again...' He hung up abruptly.

Salahudeen was shattered. He was caught in a dilemma...to choose between his principles and his emotions. On one side was his beautiful daughter in the captivity of a dreaded terrorist and on other side were his principles of truly developing Pakistan. By a strange twist of fate, he could not have both of them together. Either he compromised on his principles or forgot about his daughter. He was helpless and did not know what to do.

He asked the police commissioner whether there had been any breakthrough in tracking the caller and the place from where the calls were being made. The police commissioner looked enthusiastic for the first time since the investigation into the kidnapping had started. He told Salahudeen, 'Sir, we have now established that the caller is calling from one place only though he is changing the SIM cards. However, more importantly, we are also tracking all the calls on radio sets made in all possible frequencies. And we have intercepted some suspicious calls on radio between the place from where the ransom is being asked and another place around 40 km from Margalla National Park.'

Salahudeen was thrilled to know about this breakthrough in their investigation.

The police commissioner continued, 'Sir, we expect to close in on that place by tomorrow morning. We are sure that the kidnappers have kept Maliha there.'

Salahudeen said, 'Thank you very much commissioner. I am happy that you are finally zeroing in on the possible place where my Maliha might be held in captivity.

However, please take sufficient care to see that they do not get any hint about your presence there, otherwise Maliha's life could be in danger.'

The commissioner said, 'Sir, don't worry. The best brains in our department who have specialised in software to identify exact locations on the basis of intercepted radio signals, have been deployed on this task. We hope to get the exact coordinates of that spot by midnight today. Once we get that, immediately our three teams will leave for that place. We shall keep our vehicles far away from the exact spot to avoid giving any indications of our arrival to the kidnappers. By early morning we shall surround that place and wait for an opportune moment to attack.'

Salahudeen expressed his satisfaction over the plan. He was visibly relieved to know that his daughter was about to be traced and hopefully rescued in the next few hours.

Chapter 10

The sun rose at around 5.30 am, spreading a golden orange hue in the blue skies. Dilawar Khan woke up early and exercised. He believed in keeping his body fit. He realised that Maliha had also woken up and was watching the news on TV to know her parents' situation. Whenever visuals of her crying mother were shown, tears came to her eyes automatically. She did not know how long this ordeal was going to last. She somehow wanted to communicate with her parents and inform them that even though she was in captivity, she was safe and well taken care of. She worried even more thinking about how much her parents worried about her. But Dilawar Khan had not given her access to any phone connection from where she could contact anyone outside.

As he entered the drawing room, Maliha asked Dilawar Khan, 'Sir, you are a Muslim. You offer prayers five times a day. You have read the Quran many times, as you say. Then why are you indulging in such activities?'

Dilawar Khan did not want to answer her question. He realised, based on their previous interactions, that she would force him to think in a different way, which incidentally appeared very logical and positive in nature.

Sensing that she was expecting an answer from him, he said, 'See Maliha, I need not answer your questions. I am not even supposed to discuss anything with you. Actually you should feel grateful that we are being very nice to you. We have not harmed you in any way…'

Maliha said, 'Sorry sir, but you are on a wrong path. A true Muslim who follows the path of Islam does not inflict any injuries on others. Neither Islam nor any other religion preaches violence, killing and kidnapping. Do you think that your prayers will be answered by Allah?

Dilawar Khan was again getting drawn into a discussion. He said, 'Yes, Allah is all Merciful. He guides everyone who prays to him with a sincere heart.'

Maliha said, 'Exactly. But your deeds are not matching with the sincerity of your prayers. If you pray sincerely five times a day and commit crimes the rest of the time, I am sure Allah will not show mercy on you.'

'How do you decide what is a good deed and a bad deed?' he asked. 'Something which is good for you may not be good for others, right?'

Maliha answered, 'Agreed. But at least you need to ensure that your actions do not interfere with the freedom, happiness and progress of others. You can never classify any of your actions as good, when it puts many others in trouble.'

Dilawar Khan was thoughtful. He said, 'But we are doing this for a cause. This is only retaliation for the injustices happening to our Muslim brothers in other parts of the world.'

'Sir, you are sadly mistaken,' said Maliha. 'You have probably been excessively brainwashed in the camps where they teach you all these things. Please remember that the organisers of these camps are outlawed members of society and live a life of hatred. They always think of destruction. They are acting against the principles of Islam. Moreover, they commit bigger crimes by inducting young people like you into adopting their ideology.'

Dilawar Khan wondered how she knew about the camps, about the Organisation and brainwashing etc.

Maliha continued, 'Sir, it is never late. Please change your ways. I have watched your behaviour in school. You have a positive side to your personality. Let that flourish please. This life of hatred and destruction will not take you very far. You might have been assured that with these acts you will surely be allotted a place in Jannat. Forget Jannat, you will be sent to the worst of Jahannum.'

Now this was getting a bit too much for Dilawar Khan to handle. He found himself agreeing with every sentence spoken by Maliha. He suddenly remembered his younger days when he used to discuss these matters in their small house with all his family members. His younger sister had also argued with him on various matters and for some reason he remembered her today after so many years. It brought tears to his eyes. He wondered what they were all doing now. It was quite some time since he met with all of them. For a moment he saw his sister in Maliha and shuddered at the thought. He loved his sister very much and could not imagine a situation where she was kidnapped like Maliha.

Dilawar Khan was looking outside the window and thinking about these things when he suddenly spotted some suspicious movement near the bushes close to the road leading to the guest house. His sixth sense told him that there was danger ahead. He quickly rose to his feet and rushed into his room to fetch his revolver. Seeing this sudden move from Dilawar Khan, Maliha got panicky as she did not know what had changed so suddenly.

In the next two minutes Dilawar Khan looked through the gaps in the curtains and knew that the police teams were approaching the guest house. So, they had traced the radio calls and found the location where they had been hiding. Now he had to act fast. There was no time.

He knew very well that they would not storm and attack the guest house because they would be concerned for Maliha's life. They would also be well aware that Dilawar Khan was armed with weapons and could pose a threat to Maliha if such a situation arose. Dilawar Khan's mind was now racing. He quickly thought about all the options in front of him. One option was to surrender. Obviously, he was not very comfortable with that. He quickly called the Boss and apprised him.

The Boss was furious at this turn of events. He shouted on the phone, 'So, that Home Minister has continued to take the support of the police? I think he needs to learn his lesson. Kill Maliha…'

Dilawar Khan was stunned for a moment. He wanted to confirm that what he heard was correct. He said, 'Boss, you mean that I should kill Maliha?'

The Boss said, 'Yes, kill Maliha and escape from that place quickly. Since he has not chosen to continue the negotiations with us, there are no options left for us. What do they think of themselves? We need to be strict with these people…'

Dilawar Khan was not convinced. He said, 'Boss, but this girl is too young. She is so good natured and brilliant. What mistake has she committed that we kill her? I mean…'

Surprised, the Boss asked, 'Since when you have started seeing good and bad things in people Dilawar? In our profession, there is nothing called good and nothing called bad. We just follow orders. We never question a command. Go ahead...shoot the girl and escape.'

Dilawar Khan tried one last time, 'Boss, but is it necessary to kill the girl? Can we not…'

The Boss said, 'Dilawar, I think you need to be sent to another camp for brainwashing. It has been a long time since you were taught about our vision, mission and goals. Your life is much more important to us than Maliha's life. Kill her at once and escape. I don't want you to get into trouble with the police. Come on…fast.' The Boss hung up.

Maliha was silently listening to Dilawar's side of the conversation. She realised that her life was in danger. She did not know what to do. She was helpless.

Dilawar Khan quickly decided something in his mind. He took out his revolver and started firing outside the window near the bushes. Immediately, the security guards around the guest house were alerted and they started firing randomly, sensing some kind of a trouble. That provoked the police, who were present in large numbers and hiding behind various bushes around the house. Within a few seconds, there was a mini battle being fought there, between the police and the security guards. Maliha was shocked at this sudden unprovoked firing by Dilawar Khan.

Then Dilawar Khan aimed at Maliha and fired three times. But not a single bullet hit her. All the bullets went past her into the wall and the cupboard. She was frozen with fear. She did not know how he lost his aim. And in a sudden move, he just smiled at her with a look of compassion in his eyes and waving goodbye, ran towards the back of the guest house and jumped out from the kitchen window. Within the next few seconds, he disappeared behind the bushes.

Maliha stood inside the guest house not understanding what had really happened. She was too terrified and also somewhat confused at the turn of events.

Soon the police entered the guest house and took Maliha under their control. They asked where Dilawar was. She did not know what to say. She pointed to the bedroom window opposite the kitchen window and said, 'He ran away from there.' She did not know why she did this, but she was happy. Probably, by then she realised that Dilawar Khan had actually escaped without hurting her. His last smile was to convey to her that he had agreed to some of her viewpoints. She somehow felt obligated: since he had saved her life, she needed to save his life as well. For that reason, she diverted the police in the opposite direction. By the time they realised that they were searching for him in the wrong location, he would have got enough time to get far away from them.

In the next twenty minutes, Dilawar Khan was sitting in an intercity bus with a satisfied smile on his face. He had once again changed his appearance. The reason for the smile was that for the first time, he felt that he had done something good. He had also created an alibi which would make others believe that he actually tried to fire at Maliha but had missed due to the pressure of the fast-approaching police outside the guest house.

All the news channels started beaming Breaking News that Maliha had been rescued alive from the kidnappers and that she was safe. The news also showed the police reports that Dilawar Khan had tried to fire at Maliha just before escaping. However, he had missed.

Only Dilawar Khan and Maliha knew that he missed intentionally. It was only to make the Boss feel that he had tried to obey his orders but could not succeed.

Chapter 11

While most of the police teams immediately went looking for Dilawar Khan, one team was left behind to look after Maliha and take her back to her parents. The police asked Maliha how she was and whether she needed any medical assistance. But from her neat and tidy appearance, it was evident that Dilawar Khan had taken good care of her during her period of captivity.

Khwaja Salahudeen and his wife Razia were delighted to hear the news and were so happy to see their daughter again, unscathed after the kidnapping. The moment the police took Maliha home, there was jubilation across the country on seeing the young girl reunite with her family. Razia could not control the tears of joy flowing from her eyes as she hugged her daughter for several minutes, as if she was worried that if she released her, someone would snatch her once again from her.

The entire country erupted in joy as the news spread across. The same talk reverberated across all the lanes, markets and houses. People talked about the bravery of the girl who had managed to keep her cool during this period and never gave up. They also talked about Salahudeen's courage and how he did not yield to the demands of the kidnappers.

Over the next two days, journalists were asking Maliha many questions about the kidnapper. . She was somehow not willing to give them any clue which could have put Dilawar Khan in trouble. She had realised that while Dilawar Khan was associated with the Organisation, he had a humane side as well. She felt triumphant that through her moral talks with him repeatedly during those days, she had been able rekindle his positive side.

It was her personal victory. But she could neither show her excitement nor describe her feelings as it would have hinted to others that she had a soft corner for Dilawar Khan. This could have been misconstrued by others, and they could possibly think that she had helped him to escape from being caught by the police at that crucial time.

Khwaja Salahudeen was also feeling elated that he had not compromised his principles or ideology to get his daughter back from the jaws of the kidnappers. However, in his mind, he believed that luck had played an equally important role along with the efforts of the police department. How else could he believe the fact that in spite of being in the kidnapper's custody for a full 36 hours, his daughter had come out alive, unscathed and unhurt?

The following week in Parliament, as per a long planned schedule, a statement was to be made by the Home Minister on his ideas on developing Pakistan. He had been airing his revolutionary views occasionally on television and in the print media, but this time, he was going to address Parliament. Everyone knew that he was an intellectual and had a very progressive mind. However, in light of the recent kidnapping drama of his daughter, people were wondering whether he would go ahead with his address. People were also looking for more details on the abduction and release case. The lawmakers were all keenly looking forward to hearing the Home Minister speak on this subject. While the opposition party leaders always criticised and ridiculed Khwaja Salahudeen for many of his initiatives and accomplishments, they were secretly very impressed with his 'pure ideas'. Everyone knew that Salahudeen treated the country above everything else in his life. He was one politician who was genuinely interested in developing Pakistan. Therefore, when the Home Minister rose to his feet in the Parliament to speak, everyone was listening to him in rapt attention. And as the proceedings were telecast live, the people across the country were also eagerly looking forward to his address.

Khwaja Salahudeen said, *'Respected Speaker sir and my fellow lawmakers of Pakistan, it is with great pride and happiness I inform you all that we have successfully rescued a young girl studying in 10th standard, from the kidnappers who held her in captivity for over 36 hours. That young girl happened to be my daughter. This incident nevertheless raises a few questions which we need to ask ourselves, including myself. The first and foremost question is: are we providing adequate security to the citizens of our country? If not, then it is a matter of shame for all of us sitting here. We are the elected Government of Pakistan, who has been entrusted with the responsibility of protecting the country and its people from any kind of threat. We are supposed to devote all our energy and resources for the welfare of our people and the growth of this country.*

'I am happy to inform you that we could rescue Maliha from the kidnappers without meeting any of their demands. Their demands included giving them a lot of money and also releasing 10 dreaded terrorists, who are currently lodged in our various jails. On the personal front, I had a fight with my family about not meeting their demands. I was not in favour of meeting these demands, as it would have further emboldened them to carry out more such kidnappings in future. Moreover, releasing the terrorists was a very demoralising proposition, as it would have instantly demeaned the efforts of our brave police personnel who had risked their lives in capturing them.

'Today Pakistan is on the threshold of a new era. The world around us is changing very fast. Countries are shedding their past and embracing the future with optimism and promise. We also need to change. We cannot keep harping on the painful partition or continue to fight over a piece of land called Kashmir. What we need to do is to look at the big picture. What is the use of Kashmir, if we are not able to properly use the much

larger size of land already available with us? Are we making foreign policies just for satisfying our egos? We need to change.

'Pakistan is a blessed land. We are the sixth most populous country in the world. We have a coastline of over 1000 km, which, if utilized efficiently, can boost our maritime business activities. Our Armed Forces are the eighth largest in the world. Our heritage and culture is one of the oldest in the region. We are one of the few nuclear powers in the world. Don't these figures make us proud? Well, not in the current scenario. And the reasons are not very difficult to find.

'Today, the common impression about a politician in the mind of our citizens is that of a corrupt person, who thinks and cares only about himself. Very few of us have done something worthwhile for our people. Most of the time, we think only about filling our personal coffers, building our own portfolio of assets and furthering our personal interests. This is injustice to the people of Pakistan. We cannot and should not neglect the people of our country.

'Terrorism is gaining ground on our soil. We are not showing enough courage to tackle it for various personal and vested political reasons. Since it does not affect us directly, we do not think much about it. But out there, daily, dozens of people are losing their lives in the bomb blasts, which are occurring at very frequent intervals across our major cities. Just because we move around in bulletproof cars with full security around us, is it fair that we leave our countrymen to their fate like this? Who are we deceiving in the process? Is it really worth being a powerful personality in a weak country?

'We need to think seriously about poverty and illiteracy. These two factors are the major impediments on our path of progress. If we are not able to guarantee food and basic education to our countrymen, I think we should leave our positions of elected office at once. Just because we have won elections, it does not mean that we can relax and enjoy the fruits of our labour for five years, oblivious of the stark surroundings. Our task is

not complete till every citizen of our country is able to bear the minimum expenses of educating his children and providing them food, clothing and shelter.

'I urge you all to think about Pakistan before thinking about yourselves. Feel proud to be a part of the process of change to lift our country from this mess to a glorious future. And remember, please do not think even for a moment that you are doing charity by doing so… you are doing this for your own children's safety and well being. Of what use is your wealth, if the conditions outside on the streets of Pakistan are not safe for people to walk?

'Look at our neighbour, India. Actually we are born out of them. See how they have made progress over the same years. It is not because they are bigger than us. If we talk about size, then Singapore, Japan and Dubai are much smaller than us. India is today far ahead of us in everything. The starting line in this race for development was the same for both of us. Yet they surged forward. There are reasons for their growth and development. It is about the tolerance of their citizens to diverse ideas, it is about the vision of their leaders, and it is about the passion of their industrialists to rise...

'It is high time that we start considering India as our elder brother, seeking their guidance and support in our various endeavours. I am very sure that if our intentions are right, India will go out of the way to support us. India has already demonstrated its greatness by not attacking us even once, while we made three unsuccessful attempts to invade them. India has taught the entire world the meaning of truth and non-violence. They have demonstrated that with these two qualities alone, they could shake the rock-solid British Empire which ruled over them for 90 years. Today India is considered a giant power in the field of Information Technology. Had we not separated from them in 1947, we could have shared their growth and, if possible, contributed to it as well. After all, we are not different in any way from each other. We were one

before 1947 and became two thereafter. As if to pay the price for our deeds, the eastern part of our country was dissociated with us in 1971 to form what is now called Bangladesh. This only proves an old adage... As we sow, so we reap.

'So, dear colleagues, please join me in initiating this noble move to cleanse Pakistan of all its evils and start a new chapter. Let us take Pakistan to new heights with dignity and honour. Let us show our humble face to the world. Let our citizens be proud of their country. We may need to sacrifice many things on this path of progress, as the task is gigantic in nature. But there has to be a beginning. I have already demonstrated that I did not care for even my daughter, whom I love very much. I did not want to save my daughter at the cost of 10 terrorists roaming on Pakistani streets jeopardising the lives of hundreds of daughters of Pakistan. Thank you all....'

There was a thunderous applause from all the Members of Parliament as Khwaja Salahudeen sat down. He had very honestly put forward his thoughts. It was now up to all the Members to also think along similar lines and do something good for their country. All the major revolutions were started by a spark in someone's mind. Only time would tell, whether the spark in Salahudeen's mind had sufficient strength to ignite the minds of the Parliamentarians and chart a new path for Pakistan.

In school, Maliha too had become an iconic figure. Everyone around her looked at her with awe and inspiration. She became emboldened after this incident and freely aired her views on the development of Pakistan through various measures like good education for all, particularly the girl child etc. The youth in Pakistan considered her as a role model and were motivated by her ideology and thought process.

Chapter 12

Dilawar Khan managed to escape from the scene. But he was not sure, how long he could stay hidden. On one side there was the police behind him. And now, there was a danger of the Organisation also on his trail. He had executed the kidnapping plan exactly as per the directives of the Boss till the morning when the police arrived near the guest house. At that time, the negotiations were supposed to be 'on' between the Boss and the Home Minister. As per the ethics of the Organisation, he had kept Maliha in safe custody without harming her, all along. But his intense discussions with Maliha had changed him to some extent. Now, he started thinking about everything from a different angle. He realised that society had a good side too. This side, which was hitherto unknown to him, was appealing to him now. Actually, he had got a glimpse of the common man's world when he'd been a Physical Instructor in the school. He had been carried away by the innocence of the children and their ambitions had impressed him. He had been so happy during those days, that at times he had forgotten his main objective of joining that school. Whenever there were phone calls from the Boss, he was rudely reminded about his real mission there.

The remaining reformation happened during those few hours when he had held Maliha in captivity in the guest house. She had been so brilliant and logical in her discussions that he had had a change of mind. When she told him the true meaning of Islam and the actual duties of a Muslim as prescribed in the Quran, he had realised that he was on a very wrong track. The path on which he was heading was not destined to take him very far. The life which he lived currently was that of fear, hatred and anger. He was afraid that any time the security forces would catch him. He could not move around freely in the marketplace without taking the risk of being identified and arrested. Sometimes, he even envied the beggars in this context. He felt jealous that they were roaming freely on the streets without any inhibitions whatsoever. These feelings of hatred against law enforcement agencies and those western countries who had waged a war against terrorism had been created by the tutors in the camp. It was etched on his mind that the western countries which were cooperating with the Pakistan Government in eradicating terrorism were his enemies. Now he was wondering, what made him their enemies? What wrong had they done to him that he goes and kills innocent people around the world every now and then? This action is not justified by any logic, he thought.

He began wondering how his mindset had changed in the past few days. He did not know whether this was a good change or a bad change. But for the time being he was feeling good about being good. He had not lived this life so far as a common man in a society where he mingled with everyone and shared their joys and sorrows. Now he desperately wanted to live this kind of life.

But there was a problem. Now, the Boss would send his teams to hunt him down. The act of escaping from the guest house without hurting Maliha was not according to the Boss's original plan. Sometimes plans do change as per unexpected circumstances, but the fact was that, in spite of repeated clear instructions from the Boss to kill Maliha, he had escaped from that place without even harming her. Though he had tried to create a scene where it appeared as if he had tried to shoot her while fleeing but had missed his target, he was not sure that the Boss would believe it. During his training days, the Boss had observed the sharpness and accuracy of Dilawar Khan's shooting abilities while he was made to move in speeding vehicle with the targets being moved at different speeds in various directions. The Boss now had strong reason to suspect every action of Dilawar Khan, since he had defied the Boss's instructions to kill Maliha and had then taken his own decisions without even keeping the Boss informed about his plans. This was strictly not in accordance with the Organisation's rules and few had attempted this before. So, there was an additional threat to him now: from the Boss. In the Organisation's rules, defiance and disobedience were considered very serious offences. So, he had very limited options in front of him now.

Dilawar Khan travelled in the bus till its last stop. From there he caught another bus going towards the northern border of Pakistan. For the next two days, he travelled in buses and stayed for few hours at the bus stands. He did this to avoid being spotted by the Organisation or the police. Safety lay in a moving bus and changing buses frequently. So, if anyone noticed him and passed on the information, by the time anyone came searching for him, he would be in a totally different location, that too moving again. He wanted to live safely somewhere for a few days before he could chalk out his future strategy. And the only safe place was outside Pakistan. He was already wanted in India, so it was too risky to be in India as well.

Finally, after much deliberation he concluded that the best option for him was to hide somewhere in Nepal till the atmosphere calmed down and the heat settled down. Once the idea was firmed up in his mind, he changed his name and used a fake passport to enter Nepal via a flight to Kathmandu. He came out of the airport without being stopped or questioned by the authorities as his papers looked authentic. He stood outside the airport and took a deep breath of fresh air. He felt so happy at being free, not being chased by anyone and not being afraid of anyone. It was almost like he was reborn.

He stayed in an ordinary lodge in Kathmandu for one week during which he enjoyed his life thoroughly. The definition of the term 'enjoyment' had now changed for him. He moved freely among the crowds without any bad intentions of killing or harming someone, after so many years. Every time he had moved in crowds earlier, it was to plant a bomb or to shoot someone. And now without any such intentions, his mind was relaxed. He was enjoying the sight of shopkeepers trying to sell their wares to ladies who were looking for discounts in almost everything they bought. Everyone was busy in his/her own world. This is real life...he felt, when you have no fears or tensions of anything whatsoever.

Then he suddenly remembered that the Organisation had a small branch operating in Nepal as well, which was used mainly for infiltrating their members into India from the Nepal-India border, for carrying out specific tasks. He knew that the main business of this branch was to introduce counterfeit currency notes into India. He also realised that by being in the open like this, he was risking his life. There was every possibility that someday some member of the Organisation would recognise him. If he was recognised, then it was a matter of time before he would be caught and probably punished instantly for his defiance in the Maliha case. He was already in the bad books of the Boss and surely his men could locate him anytime.

With these thoughts, he decided to move into the interior of Nepal for some time, instead of staying in the more visible capital city. He bought a map of Nepal from a nearby stationary shop and studied the geography of Nepal in detail. He located a place called Bhaktapur on the outskirts of Kathmandu, which appeared to be safe. He vacated the lodge the very next morning and headed for Bhaktapur.

When he reached Bhaktapur, he was awed by its heritage. He observed how sometimes, the absence of technological advancements helped in preserving the serenity of a place. It was rare to find such calmness, tranquillity and peace in cities these days. Be it America, India or Japan, every city bustled with artificiality. There was no naturalness left anymore in them. Many people in the 'most developed' cities around the world never got to see a green patch around their houses or within walkable distance. Many of them never got an opportunity to see and appreciate the absolute beauty of the rising or setting sun due to the numerous tall buildings all around them. They never experienced the pleasure of an unadulterated pure breeze. They never saw the gentleness displayed by the butterflies while moving from one flower to another. They never got to hear the birds chirping at dawn and dusk. They missed out on many simple things in life which were actually far more precious, yet cost nothing. These pleasures were available free of cost and could be experienced by anyone. The only thing that one needed was to have a taste to appreciate and enjoy it.

At Bhaktapur, he booked a room in a lodge near the bus stand. He needed to stay for sometime in the lodge before he could rent out a room on long term basis. He planned to stay in Bhaktapur for a few months. It was an unassuming place and no one would suspect him to be hiding there. After whiling away the time by looking at the mountain range through the window and having a hot cup of tea, he was going through the local newspaper in a relaxed way, more to pass time than anything else. He was casually reading the classified advertisements section when his attention was drawn by a small advertisement for a job vacancy. There was a requirement for a gardener in an ashram, for tending the gardens and lawns. Dilawar Khan was prepared to work as a gardener, because the money he had carried with him while escaping from Margalla National Park was now almost exhausted and he did not have any resources to draw more money. In normal circumstances, he would have just contacted the Boss and wads of notes would have reached him in just a few hours. But currently he was in a very unusual situation. He had to take up some work somewhere to earn some money for his survival.

He went to a nearby hair-cutting saloon and got himself a fresh haircut. He removed his beard and moustache as well. Then he returned to his lodge, freshened up and put a small dot of vermilion at the centre of the eyebrows on his forehead in the Hindu style. If he was applying for a job in an ashram, the minimum requirement would be that he appeared like a Hindu.

He went to the Paramanand Ashram which was just a kilometre away from his lodge. As he entered the gates of the ashram, he realised that it was a big compound with sprawling lawns and lots of trees and bushes. He was excited at the thought of living in these natural surroundings. He could hear bhajans playing in a low volume which made the environment very pleasant. He found the administrative office near the entrance and went inside. He told them that he had come in response to their advertisement for the vacancy of a gardener. They asked him to wait in the office and offered him a chair to sit. A boy came from somewhere and offered him a glass of water. He was happy to be treated in this manner in a strange place. For some reason, he was attracted to this ashram and its surroundings.

Soon, a man wearing a kurta pyjama made from plain white cloth appeared and took him to an adjacent room that had one table and two chairs. The person identified himself as Swami Haridas, the Administration Manager of the ashram.

Swami Haridas asked Dilawar Khan, 'So, you have come to work here as a gardener? What is your name?'

Dilawar Khan thought for a while. He said, 'Sir, my name is Ramakrishna.'

Swami Haridas asked, 'Where are you from Ramakrishna? And what do you know about gardening?'

Dilawar Khan answered, 'Sir, we hail from North India, but have been settled in Kathmandu for the last twenty years. I was very small when my father migrated here. I learnt about gardening mostly through experience. I used to take lot of interest in trees and plants since my childhood.'

Swami Haridas asked, 'Ok, please tell me, what are considered as the essential rules of gardening?'

Dilawar Khan replied, 'Sir, watering the plants is the first and foremost requirement. The water requirements of different plants are different. Some need standing water, while some plants need to be watered twice a day. In addition we need to provide fertiliser in the right quantity. Sunlight provides the remaining requirements. We need to support the trees while they grow, till they are able to stand up by themselves. For bushes and lawns, we need to trim them periodically to ensure that they continue looking attractive and good.'

Swami Haridas was satisfied at this simple explanation of the basics of gardening.

He asked, 'Ramakrishna, what are your hobbies?'

Dilawar Khan said, 'Sir, I have no hobbies as such. Poor people cannot afford to have hobbies. However, I have developed hobbies which do not cost money. I love to watch the sunrise and sunset. Even if I watch it continuously for several days, I never get bored of it. Similarly, I like the look and feel of the greenery of grass. It is such a pleasure to walk barefoot on wet grass. I like the chirping sound of birds when they are hurrying home after a day's work comprising mainly of collecting food for their children in their nests. I find the finest melody in those sounds. I like the cool breeze of natural air. It has a very fresh and different aroma and enlightens my soul instantly.'

Swami Haridas was highly impressed with this poetic description of Ramakrishna's hobbies so easily found in natural surroundings. For a second, he felt guilty that he had actually never experienced the feelings expressed by Ramakrishna, though he lived in an environment where there was so much natural beauty. He decided within himself to start experiencing these pleasures henceforth.

Swami Haridas asked, 'Tell me about your family?'

Dilawar Khan said with a shy expression, 'Sir, I am still a bachelor. My father is looking for some good alliances for me. He wants to get me married by next year.'

Satisfied with the interview, Swami Haridas finally asked, 'So Ramakrishna, how much salary are you looking for?'

Dilawar Khan replied, 'Sir, I am ready for whatever amount you give me as salary. I am not after money. Money does not buy happiness. I want to spend the rest of my life just being in a pure environment like this and be blessed by hearing the valuable discourses of various saints at the ashram. I have no more desires left for me in life…'

Swami Haridas thought that this particular answer must have been a slight exaggeration, but chose to ignore it seeing the look of innocence on Ramakrishna's face.

Finally, they decided about the terms and conditions of his employment. Swami Haridas informed him that his salary would be Nepalese Rupees 5000/- per month. In addition he would be given accommodation at the ashram. He would be given food along with all other staff in the ashram. There was no annual leave. However, if any staff was ill, or needed medical attention, there was a visiting doctor who would provide free consultations and medication at the ashram's cost. Dilawar Khan was more than happy at these employment terms. He was asked to join the ashram the very next day, to which he agreed.

Dilawar Khan came with his suitcase to the ashram and accommodated himself in the room allotted to him. The room had a small cot and a cupboard. He had purchased a pair of white clothes for himself, to appear in sync with the surrounding staff. He was relieved for some time at least from being tracked by the members of the Organisation, who would never in their wildest dreams imagine that Dilawar Khan would have holed up in an ashram.

Dilawar Khan thoroughly enjoyed his daily routine. He woke up every morning at 5am to the sound of melodious bhajans reverberating in a low volume in the serene atmosphere of the ashram. Religious music early in the morning is bound to lift anyone's spirits in a positive manner. He quickly finished his daily ablutions and had a light breakfast prepared in the ashram's kitchen. He would then go about his job of looking after the trees and plants. His lunchtime was not fixed, but usually he had lunch sometime around 1pm. He was required to work till 5pm.

Within a week of joining the ashram, Dilawar Khan got assimilated into the ashram environment. Everyone around him liked him and enjoyed talking to him. He was very guarded, not revealing his true past to anyone. At times, circumstances forced him to make false statements, which he did with ease.

He was observing nature from such close quarters for the first time in his life. He remembered some trees planted near his childhood house in Pakistan, around which he used to play as a child. They were fruit bearing trees, and they had all had much fun climbing the trees and plucking the fresh fruits. But now, he was interacting with the trees in a totally different role. He was mentoring the trees to grow. His role was that of a guardian of trees. He felt responsible for every tree in the ashram and looked after them with great care.

He was absolutely thrilled to see new flowers blooming on the bushes every day. He wondered at Mother Nature's ability to create such magic every day. The flowers were tender, soft, colourful and aromatic. No amount of advancement in technology could ever create such natural flowers with such beautiful fragrances. On this point, technology would never score over Nature. He started believing that even plants have a life of their own. Every flower emerges as a bud, blooms for a day or two and then withers away. He felt sad while sweeping the dead, fallen leaves and flowers every morning from under the trees. He compared them with the lives of human beings. Human beings too appear in this world as tiny infants, and then they grow multiple times in size to become adults. They shrink towards their old age and then wither away one fateful day. It was a rule of Nature that a flower cannot bloom permanently all the time. Similarly, every person has his own bloom time in this world. After that, some other people come on the scene and become the centre of attraction. And the cycle goes on...

He also remembered reading a poem in his school about the fate of the flowers. Some flowers get the privilege of being part of a garland adoring the Gods or deities, while some flowers had the honour of being laid on the dead bodies of martyrs. Some flowers had the fortune of being pinned to the hair of beautiful women, while some flowers had the opportunity to be offered as a symbol of expressing love between two lovers. And the less fortunate among them remained on a tree or plant during their entire bloom period and then withered and fell down one day. Even these flowers did a wonderful job of beautifying the tree for that day. These flowers did not mind when their nectar was sucked by the honey bees. How flexible and selfless these flowers were…

Whenever he planted new saplings, he took care of them as if they were small children and even talked to them. He ensured that the saplings had good support and watered them carefully. He knew that excessive watering was detrimental to some trees. Every morning he went around each of the saplings to see its growth, its height, the formation of any new leaves and appearance of new buds. At every sign of growth, he would get thrilled and a deep satisfaction would prevail upon him.

He was living an almost content life amidst these natural surroundings. Sometimes, in the evenings, he attended the religious discourse by Swami Paramanand or other swamis. He was impressed by the fine values contained in their preaching. Many of the discourses were recited in a story form with intermittent music and religious songs which lifted the spirits of the listeners. He realised that Hindu mythology was very vast and several anecdotes reflected some value or the other.

One day he heard a discourse on the epic, Mahabharata. The subject for that day was about the 'Agyaatvas' of the Pandavas. One condition for losing the game of gambling was that the five Pandava brothers were required to stay incognito for a period of one year. And if the identity of anyone of them was revealed during that year, they would have to start afresh by counting the period all over again. The five brothers were wise and mighty, each one of them bestowed with some special quality associated with bravery and skill. It was not an easy task for them, nor was it honourable considering that they disguised themselves as cooks, servants, etc., but they valued their words more than anything. Consequently, just to honour their commitment, they did so, putting aside their egos. And Arjun had to disguise himself as a eunuch called Brihannada, wearing women's clothes. Arjun was the best archer of his time, yet he accepted this ordeal just to protect their honour and value of their commitments.

For a moment, Dilawar Khan thought that, in a way, he too was in Agyaatvas. He too was living in a disguise as a gardener. He laughed at himself. Not too long ago, he was a dreaded terrorist who had killed several people worldwide. And today, he had taken shelter inside a nondescript ashram in Nepal, just to hide from the police as well as the Organisation. He did not know how long he would live like this. Nevertheless, he was enjoying this lifestyle thoroughly.

Dilawar Khan now started taking interest in the evening discourses by various swamis from the ashram as well as by those who were invited from outside to give sermons to enlighten the people. One day there was a discourse on the 'Soul'. That day he learnt many new things about the soul.

He discovered that as per the Bhagwad Gita, the soul in every living being is the same. That meant that the soul of a snake, a tiger, a housefly, an elephant, a dog, a horse and a human being is the same. There are several species of aquatic animals which are found at the bottom of deep oceans where even sunlight does not reach. These animals take birth in that darkness and die in that darkness. No one ever sees them and they do not get to see anyone. Even their soul is the same. The soul was the driver of the body. Once the soul leaves the body, we call it a 'dead body'. After death, the physical body remains the same but it cannot 'live' because its driver, the 'soul' has departed from the body. The soul then enters another body as per its deeds in its previous incarnation. So, a person doing bad deeds in this life may reincarnate as a fish or a bird or anything else. Similarly, if a person does exceptionally good deeds, then his soul leaves this merry-go-round of appearance and disappearance in various types of species and merges with the Super Soul called Paramatma.

The goal of every soul is to try and escape this cycle of birth and death repeatedly, by escaping from this orbit. To achieve this, one needs to continuously do good deeds. Every birth comes with some miseries associated with it. The miseries get compounded if the person gets carried away in the pleasures of material indulgences because such pleasures are often transient and ephemeral. The person is tempted to commit immoral deeds just to satisfy his quest for such pleasures. That alone brings about his downfall. Once a person understands the philosophy of life and is able to experience the pleasure gained by spiritual enlightenment, he is most likely to follow a righteous path and desist from doing anything which is immoral or unethical. The happiness experienced by such people is pure, long-lasting and very satisfying. A person generally does not look elsewhere to seek happiness once he tastes spiritual contentment. Then he lives in a state of bliss.

One day, the topic of discussion for the sermon was about 'Sins and Expiation'. The swami said, 'In routine day to day life, people are bound to commit some sin or the other. Many times they do not even know that they have committed a sin. For example, when people walk on the grass, they do not know that they often crush tiny insects under their feet. What right do people have to abruptly end the life of this seemingly harmless creature enjoying itself in the green grass? We have to pay a price for every sin committed by us in our life knowingly or unknowingly.'

Dilawar Khan had been listening very passionately to this highly philosophical discourse. He asked, 'Swamiji, are all types of sins considered equal? I mean, if a person commits a sin unknowingly, will he get the same punishment as he would get when he commits a sin intentionally? Is there any way to avoid punishment for sins committed?'

Swamiji paused for a while and said, 'If a sin is committed unknowingly, then it comes with a lesser punishment and it can also be expiated. But more than that, the realisation that the sin has been committed is in itself a positive step forward. Many people today knowingly continue to commit sins after sins. They will never be pardoned in the court of God. They will get the appropriate punishment commensurate with the sins committed by them. And if the quantum of punishment exceeds their current lifetime, the punishment even extends into their next life. That is why, you find some people living an honest life, yet they suffer. Often, these people suffer because they are paying for their sins committed in their previous Janma. However, those who realise their mistakes and make genuine efforts to mend their ways and choose a right path in their life are often pardoned by God. After all what are God's qualities? God symbolises Love, Happiness, Faith and Forgiveness. God will definitely forgive anyone who sincerely tries to correct himself during any stage in his life.'

Dilawar Khan had got his answers. He had committed several sins in his past life. He did not want to commit any more crimes. He wanted to expiate his sins as much as possible in this life itself. Who knew what he would be in his next birth? And he may never get an opportunity to correct himself. It was never late to start good work in life.

And then Swamiji narrated the story of a fisherman called Valya who used to rob passersby on a lonely road outside the city near a jungle. One day, God passed by that road disguised as a Brahmin. As usual Valya stopped him and threatened to loot and kill him. The Brahmin just smiled and said, 'Please go home and ask your wife and children whether they are willing to share your sins.' He also committed to Valya that he would wait for him to come back. Valya went home and said to his wife and children, 'See, I rob and kill people just so that I earn enough money to look after you. Would you be willing to share my sins?' He was shocked to hear his wife and children tell him flatly, 'No. It is your duty to look after us. But which way you earn the money to look after us is your problem. If there are any sins attached with your deeds, we shall not be willing to share them.' Valya returned to the jungle very dejected and told the Brahmin what his wife and children had said to him. Then God, in the disguise of a Brahmin advised him, 'You come into this world alone and you go from here alone. You are the only owner of your sins and no one will share them with you. Similarly the blessings accrued due to your good deeds will come only to you and no one else.' This opened Valya's eyes and he abandoned his wrongful acts of robbing and killing people. In due course of time, he became an extremely wise and knowledgeable person known as Sage Valmiki who wrote the epic, 'Ramayana'.

Dilawar Khan was highly motivated and inspired by this story. He saw some glimpses of himself in the fisherman, Valya who had committed sins earlier, but was subsequently enlightened. Now he wanted to reform his ways and do as many good deeds as possible. He realised that the blessings of others were an invaluable asset which could never be measured in money. They had the power to have a highly positive impact on him in his remaining life as well as his next life. He vowed to himself to be a good person hereafter.

It had been almost three months since he had joined the ashram. He had adjusted himself to this plain and simple life. His thought process became gradually purified because of the pure and simple food served there. It is said that one's thoughts are largely influenced by the food one eats and the company one keeps. In his case, both these factors were highly positive and he started generating positive thoughts. He started believing in positive traits like forgiveness, kindness, peace, happiness etc. He even randomly wondered whether he would spend the rest of his life in the ashram. It was not a bad idea.

Then one day…as he was working in the garden looking after a newly planted sapling, he observed a shadow of someone standing behind him. He turned around and...he almost froze in horror. His heart skipped a beat. A chill crawled up his spine. Standing there with a vicious smile on his face was…the Boss.

Dilawar Khan felt too weak to run away. He could barely stand. He wondered how the Boss had appeared here. How did he know that he was hiding here? He had no answer. The only thing he knew was that he was in deep trouble.

Chapter 13

Yashwant had no information nor any clue about Dilawar Khan's whereabouts or what he was doing. Nevertheless, he did not give up on his mission and continued to 'Visualise and Believe' that Dilawar Khan was a reformed person. He religiously carried on with this exercise of ordering his sub-conscious mind to reform Dilawar Khan, every day for at least 15 minutes. He knew that one day or the other he would see the results of his efforts. But he had no idea when he was destined to see the results. In spite of having successfully tried and tested the theory of using the powers of his sub-conscious mind for many other things, when it came to Dilawar Khan, he doubted whether he was practicing this technique correctly. His feeling stemmed from the fact that, even after several months of effort, there was no headway or a breakthrough in this matter. Yet, his mind was telling him that although he had no information about Dilawar Khan, there was a distinct possibility that he was getting reformed and he would eventually come to know about it one day or the other.

Yashwant had actively remained in touch with many of his batch mates from Yogeshwar's camp. And he met some of them almost on a weekly basis. They would all get inspired by seeing one another using the technique for a variety of causes. By sharing their experiences, he realised that they had used this concept successfully for many important purposes. One of them had used it for locating a suitable house for rent, which matched with their exact requirements. This is generally a difficult task, as every member of the house has different priorities regarding the quality of house required. The lady of the house prefers a house which is nearer to the market and is in a good neighbourhood, while the children want a park near the house. The house also has to be near the bus/local station for an easy commute. The ventilation has to be good and most importantly, the budget needs to match as well. Therefore, to get a house which met everyone's demands is rarely found in normal life.

One of them even used it for finding a suitable marriage alliance for his daughter. This was a very sensitive and delicate Issue as getting a groom acceptable to the girl and her parents is also somewhat difficult to come across these days. The parents generally tend to look for a groom with good social status and a stable job from a traditional family, while the daughters gives more priority to the other parameters like looks, compatibility, outlook etc. The children of today's generation are more open to seeking these details and do not mind rejecting proposals if they are not too comfortable with the proposal. They prefer to wait rather than accept something blindly.

Such inspiring stories motivated them to continue using this technique for anything and everything worthwhile that they desired in life. A sceptical person would always say that all these incidents, where the desired goals were achieved, were just a matter of sheer coincidence and a figment of the imagination. But for these people who practiced it sincerely and believed in it, this was nothing short of the successful tapping into the gigantic storehouse of power of their sub-conscious minds.

One day, Yashwant thought that apart from continuing to try this theory on Dilawar Khan, why did he not test it on something which was achievable but somewhat difficult, and which may not happen otherwise? This would eliminate any doubts in his mind about whether his sub-conscious mind's power was fading away or was still intact like earlier, when he derived positive results by practicing it. And he actively started thinking about what he should aspire for. He realised that, for a long time now, he had wanted to lose weight. It might seem silly, but apart from sportspersons and cinema actors who can lose and gain weight as and when required through rigorous exercise cum diet regimes, for an ordinary person, it is still a distant dream. Many people desperately want to lose weight but cannot do so for various reasons. In reality, Yashwant's body had been in perfect shape all these years but off late, with age catching up, he was not really doing strenuous exercises like jogging or gymming, and confined himself to some 'light' activities like walking, Yoga and few bending and stretching exercises. A person nearing fifty finds it difficult to retain the zeal of continuing to exercise just to keep his body trim and fit, as he knows very well that he can never regain the youthful looks of his twenties at any cost. As a result, he had put on weight and was slightly overweight by the Body Mass Index criteria. He had thought of taking some steps to reduce his weight but all his thoughts had remained only thoughts. And only-thoughts-without-actions have no value. The main reason why he was not able to turn his ideas into action was that he felt lazy to get up early in the morning.

For most people in this world, getting up early in the morning is the biggest challenge of their lives. They do so only forcibly, when they have to catch a flight or a train early in the morning. Waking up early was the singlemost factor that most often separated successful people from the 'rest of the crowd' in this world. Actually, no one likes to get up early in the morning after a deep sleep. But then, people with a mission, people with a clear goal in front of their eyes do get up and get going with their tasks. And usually these people succeed in their lives. He now wanted to test whether his powers of the sub-conscious mind would make that 'change' happen in him.

Yashwant told himself, 'If this works, then it is the ultimate test to confirm that the powers of my sub-conscious mind are still intact. Let me see whether my own reluctance can be warded off just by my positive thinking and by channelizing the powers of my sub-conscious mind in the right direction. So, he started the exercise. He began visualising that *he had a trim figure. His shoulders were slightly wider and his chest had come out while his stomach went in. He had a spring in his step. He looked firm and walked with confidence. He was looking at himself with self-admiration in a full-size mirror.* He started practicing the technique every evening with these visuals in his mind and believed that this was going to happen soon. The belief was a must in this process.

The following week, when Yashwant came back from office, he found a couple sitting in their living room with his wife. They introduced themselves as their new neighbours, Mr. and Mrs. Kripalani. After a brief discussion on various topics, they started talking about how pleasant the weather was. Kripalani mentioned that he was a 'walking freak'. He expressed his excitement at the refreshing weather and the sheer joy of going for morning walks. He casually invited Yashwant to join him on his morning walks. Yashwant readily accepted the invitation knowing full well that he had to cross the first hurdle of getting up earlier than normal.

After just three days of conscious effort to get up early in the morning, Yashwant made the biggest discovery of his lifetime: that only the first three minutes after the clock sounds the 'wake up alarm' are extremely crucial. If a person can conquer these three minutes, then he can achieve anything in his life. He is absolutely ready to face any challenge and take on any responsibility in his life. Once he walks up to the bathroom and puts the toothbrush in his mouth, the battle was already half won.

Just the realisation of the immense benefits of 'waking up early in the morning and going for a brisk walk in fresh air' is enough to drive the person thereafter. He also realised that when a person went alone for morning walks, there were chances that he would miss the routine more often, rather than if he went with friends. Because, when one goes for morning walks with friends, automatically there is a kind of commitment and one does not skip it except in case of genuine emergencies. So, within just two weeks of initiating the process, Yashwant found that he was regularly going out for morning walks with Kripalani.

It was during this period that he happened to read a motivational book which said that there is always something called a 'Private Victory' and then a 'Public Victory'. The private victory is when the person commits himself to do something and achieves it. The public victory is when the person achieves success in his profession or in his field of passion. And invariably, the private victory usually preceded the public victory. Rarely would you find someone who has achieved a public victory without achieving the private victory first. One of the surest forms of measuring the private victory is to regularly go for morning walks, as it raises a person's self confidence, self esteem and motivational levels apart from the myriad physical benefits to his body.

After a few days, Yashwant noticed that a new gym had opened just opposite his house and that they were offering a flat 50% discount on membership for the first hundred customers. There was an additional discount of 25% for a second person from the same family. His wife was very interested in joining the gym because three of her friends had also joined it within one week of its inauguration. This is one more thing with women all over the world. If they see one or more of their friends doing something, they need to do it as well. So, it was but natural that she joined the gym too. Once she knew that there was a further discount for a second membership, Yashwant was immediately roped in by his wife to avail the discount. Yashwant observed that this was one more of his wife's characteristics. She would buy something just because there was a discount, knowing fully well that she did not need that item or may not use it in her lifetime. Nevertheless, thanks to his wife he started going to the gym regularly. Under the guidance of a professional trainer, he started doing physical workouts on various machines after a gap of almost six years. And he was feeling better and better as he continued with his new schedule.

And then he came home one day to find that his wife had learnt new recipes for making several delicious dishes using healthy ingredients like oats, whole wheat, wheat bran etc. His wife was someone who always tried cooking new items and enjoyed cooking healthy food by using less oil. This is one of the biggest blessings along with equivalent risks for any husband in the world. If the wife is a cooking freak, she will keep testing and trying out new dishes and the husband has no choice but to eat everything with a smile on his face and appreciate the new taste. No woman would like to hear her husband say that the new dish, prepared so enthusiastically by her, has not come out well. So, this newfound adventure of his wife resulted in a very nutritious diet being served up for breakfast, lunch and dinner. Yashwant was happy with this healthy diet because it tasted genuinely delicious. So, it was a win-win situation wherein he got taste and health simultaneously. Otherwise, generally speaking, all that tastes good is generally not good for health and vice versa.

All these factors resulted in gradually transforming Yashwant's body into a with perfectly toned physique. It took all of just three months for Yashwant to realise his long-cherished dream to find himself in a physically fit and trim figure. It was not as if he could not have done all this earlier. But he was not getting enough push to start off. In such endeavours, a good start is required to endure continuance.

It is debatable whether all these events like the Kripalanis becoming their new neighbours, the opening of the new gym near their house with grand discounts and the trying out of new healthy recipes by his wife were all because of the powers of his sub-conscious mind. But one thing was clear...these things started happening when he started practicing the technique.

Similarly, the things external to us combine in a well-orchestrated manner to make us realise our belief by using this technique. There could be millions of coincidences, but coincidences do happen. If we are able to make coincidences happen, then why not try and attempt something that we desire? It is for people who have faith and belief to try out. The others simply disbelieve and miss out on using the huge reservoir of powers available to them.

He was now more resolved in his belief to see Dilawar Khan reformed. He was sure that very soon he would find Dilawar Khan reformed.

Chapter 14

The Boss and Dilawar Khan were sitting in Dilawar Khan's room in the ashram drinking hot tea. During their discussions Dilawar Khan learnt that the Boss had been informed about his presence in the ashram by one of his gang members working in Nepal. The Boss had then decided to come to Nepal because he wanted to talk to Dilawar Khan personally. To be in close proximity with Dilawar Khan, the Boss had taken up the role of a contractor constructing a small room in the ashram. Apart from their continuous surveillance on Dilawar Khan, the Organisation's members were posted outside the ashram to ensure that he did not attempt any tricks to escape from their radar this time. It was ironical that the Organisation had to monitor and watch the activities of one of their senior members, Dilawar Khan. After Dilawar Khan had left the kidnapping scene by defying the Boss' instructions, The Boss had thought a lot about Dilawar Khan's intentions and actions. The Boss had been furious then that Dilawar Khan had escaped without hurting Maliha and moreover defied his instructions so blatantly. He'd been curious to understand Dilawar's thought process that had made him to this. As a principle, he always listened to both sides of an argument before arriving at any conclusion, which was a rare quality among people of his kind.

The Boss asked Dilawar Khan, 'So Dilawar, tell us now, what made you to run away from the kidnapping scene by defying my orders? Were you not afraid to defy my orders and escape just like that? How could you ever imagine in your wildest dreams that you could escape and continue to lead a happy life without us finding you?'

Dilawar Khan had no ready answers to give to the Boss. And whatever logical answer he had in his mind about 'morality', 'humanity' etc was beyond the Boss's comprehension anyway. He just said, 'Boss, please forgive me, but I was emotionally carried away. That girl Maliha was so brilliant and lively you know, she knew so much about politics, religion, ethics, morals etc...'

The Boss looked surprised. He said, 'What? You were emotionally carried away? Since when did you start having emotions, Dilawar? Where were your emotions when you killed hundreds of innocent people in several bomb explosions in various countries all these years?'

Dilawar Khan tried once again to explain his logic to the Boss. He said, 'See Boss, in everyone's life, there comes a turning point when one hears a voice from within. I heard one such voice asking me to forsake all activities which harmed people. I wanted to lead a good life where I need not be afraid of the police, and also where people were not afraid of me. I had a strong urge to mingle with common people and be a part of society'.

The Boss said, 'See Dilawar, you are a very good person. We have trained you extensively and prepared you for certain tasks. We are proud of your achievements so far. You have successfully completed all the tasks assigned to you so far, with remarkable precision and great accuracy. You were being groomed to take up some bigger positions with higher responsibilities in the Organisation. Then why did you change all of a sudden?'

Dilawar Khan did not know what to say. He said, 'Boss, I deeply respect you and also have very high regard for you. You are the one who gave me an entity and an image in the Organisation. I learnt so many things under your guidance. But now, I am a changed person. My priorities in life have changed. I am no longer interested in killing people, kidnapping, assaults etc. This creates an environment of fear and hatred among innocent people in society. I want to contribute positively to society. I can do that by being good myself, and not by continuing in the way I had worked in the Organisation all these years.'

The Boss looked at Dilawar Khan with pity. He said, as if speaking to a child, 'Look Dilawar, you seem to be under some kind of a fleeting influence. What you are saying is the language of a coward. You are talking like a person who shies away from his responsibilities. Life is meant to be lived like a king. One should strive to become powerful and give justice to the oppressed section of society.'

Dilawar Khan thought for a while and said, 'Sorry Boss, but I tend to disagree with you on this particular point. I am not under any temporary influence of anyone. These thoughts have been shaped in my mind over the last few months. Talking about being a coward or being brave, again I feel that the way we both define these terms is different. A person who carries illegal weapons with him and runs from place to place to hide from the law is not brave, but actually a coward. Bravery is to stand up for a cause acceptable to the larger sections of society. Such a person can be called a real king, not the one who operates through hideouts. Lastly, who has given us the power and the authority to dispense justice to others? There are judicial systems in every country which are supposed to take care of their citizens. We are not authorized by anyone to be the judge and give out judgments.'

The Boss was slowly losing his cool now. He firmly said, 'Dilawar, you are a child in front of me. I have spent a lifetime pursuing my ideology and carrying out my operations all over the world. Do you think you will change me by such talks? I can only pity you…'

'Boss, please do not misunderstand me. I am too small to advise you or even give you any suggestions. But I sincerely feel that we all should change ourselves before it is too late. We may not get an opportunity to correct ourselves tomorrow...'

The Boss looked at Dilawar Khan helplessly. 'I am sorry Dilawar, but the way you are talking and preaching I am reminded about that dreadful disease called cancer. Do you know what doctors do when they detect cancer in a patient? They try to cut off the affected part from the main body. It seems painful, but that is the only cure, otherwise the cancer spreads slowly inside the entire body. Similarly, if we allow you to go scot free with your ideology, tomorrow there would be ten more of our members who would dare to speak the same language and leave the Organisation. But let me tell you one thing clearly, there is no way one leaves the Organisation. The only time a member leaves our Organisation is...when he dies. The death could be either a natural death or an accidental death or an encounter... There may be many ways to enter our Organisation, but only one way to leave it...' The Boss pointed his index finger upwards as he spoke the last sentence.

Dilawar Khan was now worried. He had very few options before him. Still, he persisted in taking his argument further by saying, 'Boss, I do not mind if you call me a cancer, but please think. I sincerely feel that the Organisation is on the wrong path. The road on which we all are going will only lead to self-destruction. It will do no good to either the Organisation or to anyone else. Because of our actions, hundreds of innocent lives are lost every year all over the world. What right do we have to take someone's life? The Merciful Allah never advised anyone to harm someone, for any reason whatsoever. For every issue, there is a possible peaceful resolution. No one should take the law into his own hands in a civilised society. In fact, on the Day of Judgment, we are mandatorily required to answer for all our deeds, both good as well as bad. And you know very well, what happens to those people whose deeds are found to be unclean.'

The Boss was now quite angry. He said curtly, 'Look Dilawar, I suspect now that by staying for a few days in this ashram, you have lost your sense of balanced thinking. You are becoming insane. I give you time till tomorrow. Please think it over. I have an important assignment lined up for you. I need your expertise in that. This could probably be the most important assignment so far in your life and your career with the Organisation. And yes, do not try any gimmicks of escaping from here. The entire area surrounding the ashram is now under my surveillance round the clock. You cannot go out without being noticed by us. And I have already instructed my people to shoot you down, in case they find you trying to escape. So, don't try anything funny, ok? Now sleep peacefully and let us conclude our discussions tomorrow morning. Good night…'

Dilawar Khan meekly said, 'Good night Boss…'

That night, Dilawar Khan could not sleep. A huge storm was brewing in his mind and he was unable to think properly. He had spent his entire childhood in abject poverty and a state of deprivation. He had indulged in several anti-social activities during his teenage years. He had become a certified terrorist at a very young age. He had killed several people in bomb blasts and shootouts. However, since the time he had been caught in India and lodged in the Mumbai jail, the circumstances around him had changed dramatically. First, it was Yashwant who had tried to reform him and then it was Maliha who had shared some very upright thoughts with him. Now, he was almost reformed. He wanted to lead a life of simplicity. And suddenly, with the unexpected arrival of the Boss on the scene, he was compelled to go back to his old life of crime. He did not want to indulge in crime again. But the Boss was serious. He meant business. He would not hesitate to eliminate Dilawar Khan if he suspected any disobedience or defiance from him this time.

Dilawar Khan did not know when he slept off that night. He had kept thinking about the options in front of him and how to extricate himself from this precarious situation.

The next day morning, he woke up with a clear mind. He was relieved at finally taking a decision. The storm inside his mind was over. He was feeling very light.

As he went about his daily chores in the garden, the Boss came up to him and asked him, 'So Dilawar, what have you decided?'

Dilawar Khan said calmly, 'Boss, I have thought it over. You were right. I was mistaken and was on a wrong path. I do not know what prompted me to tread that path, but then, it happened.'

The Boss was confused.

Dilawar Khan continued, 'I was misguided for some time into believing that the life of simplicity would give me happiness. But now I realise that I was mistaken. There is no fun in living a life in which there is no thrill and excitement. Such a life is lead by only the cowards in this world. I have been trained well by the Organisation. I want to use my skills suitably. I am ready for the new assignment.'

The Boss could not control his excitement. He patted Dilawar's shoulder and hugged him. He said, 'Very good. That's like a good boy. I am proud of you, Dilawar. I knew that you would change. These temporary feelings of being good or being noble cannot sustain in the minds of people like us for a long time, who are used to living a life of thrills and excitement. You have made me proud today… now listen carefully; your new assignment is still in the planning stage. But it is a grand plan…we plan to crash two planes in India. One on Parliament and one on the Bombay Stock exchange. We want to paralyse India…'

Dilawar Khan was stunned to hear this plan. It was indeed a very big plan, one that was hatched only once in a decade or so. He feebly asked, 'What is my role in this, Boss?'

The Boss looked into his eyes and coldly said, 'You will be the hijacker cum suicide bomber in one of the planes. You will die with the plane when it crashes…'

Dilawar Khan was shocked to know that his death had been planned by the Boss. Seeing his sudden change of expressions, the Boss said, 'Dilawar, do you remember the moral training we imparted to you in your early days in the camp? When you die while fulfilling a mission, you get a sure place in the Jannat. The time has come for you to make this supreme sacrifice in your life. I am sure you would not hesitate to discharge your duties at this crucial moment. I have full faith in you.'

Dilawar Khan felt as though the floor under his feet was slipping away. In his earlier days, he had been brainwashed into thinking that death while executing a mission was a very honourable act. However, that was then. Now he had changed. Now he wanted to live. He did not want to die so soon. He did not say anything.

The Boss continued, 'We are camping with you till the plan is finally ready for implementation in a month or two. Now please continue to do your work as a gardener with the same concentration as before, so that others do not suspect us. Bye…' Soon, the Boss left the ashram.

Dilawar Khan's mind was working overtime. He wondered at his fate. He thought, 'What an irony. When I was in a jail in Mumbai, Yashwant was trying very hard to reform me. At that time I had acted as if I was getting reformed. But within me I knew that I was bad. I was actually waiting for an opportunity to escape. And today, the circumstances are exactly the opposite. Now I am actually reformed and the Boss is trying to 're-reform' me. I am now acting as though I have become bad again but within me I know that I am not bad now. Once again, and probably for the last time, I am just waiting for an opportunity to escape!'

Chapter 15

Ever since Dilawar Khan had heard about the new assignment he had been worrying as to how he could avoid being involved in it. He also worried about how he could stop the Boss from executing the plan. He did not want to see India getting harmed at any cost. He believed that India was a great country. It had a rich culture and one of the oldest heritages. In fact, there had been no Pakistan before 1947. So, basically, Pakistan had no right to fight with India, as it had been formed out of India. How can a child fight with his parent ever? He realised that Pakistan was being foolish in waging war with India and nurturing terrorists who fought against India on its soil.

For the first time, Dilawar Khan agreed with Khwaja Salahudeen. Salahudeen was desperately trying to develop Pakistan. He had a vision to ensure that Pakistan's well-being was in development and not in trying to engage in continual skirmishes with India. Pakistan also had a right to progress to become a prosperous nation. Why should the people of Pakistan suffer because of the apathy of their corrupt politicians? Why should they lead a life of abject poverty and unending misery, when the country was actually bestowed with so many natural resources like fertile lands, numerous rivers, and vast mineral deposits?

If Pakistan really developed, then there would be no more Dilawar Khans born from the underprivileged sections of society. He suddenly recalled his family and had a strong desire to meet them one last time before his last mission. He remembered that, despite their abject poverty, his father had never lost his zeal in following a righteous path. His mother had always tried to ensure that there was peace and harmony in the house with whatever little they had. His brothers and sisters used to play around the house with the neighbouring children oblivious of the financial sufferings of their parents. He felt that those had been happy days in his life.

However, in the subsequent years, life had taken him on a very different path. He had travelled a road which had not been travelled by many in the past. And the road did not go a long distance. It ended soon. He wondered, in spite of knowing this now, how and why he had joined the path and travelled on it till he had been reformed by a series of incidents? He had no answer. One cannot erase his past. In fact, being unable to change the past is mankind's biggest limitation.

He now wanted to mend his ways and lead a peaceful life. But the chances of that happening were very grim. He had two forces that prevented him from leading such a life. The Boss had already given him an ultimatum. The other force was that of the law. Security agencies of multiple countries were on his trail and whenever they succeeded in catching him, they would definitely punish him. In all probability, his punishment would be either death or life imprisonment.

Over the next six weeks, the Boss planned every minute detail of the attack along with Dilawar Khan. Dilawar Khan was a passive participant in those meetings, but was forced to appear enthusiastic and sincerely involved in the mission. The plan was to crash two planes, one on the Indian Parliament and the other on the Bombay Stock exchange with a gap of 15 to 20 minutes.

The plane chosen to crash into the Indian Parliament was to originate from Kathmandu. It was a Kathmandu-Delhi flight. Dilawar Khan would be part of a group who would hijack the plane immediately after its take off. They would be armed with weapons. It was easier to board flights with weapons from Kathmandu, as security systems were lax and also they could be bribed easily. This was clearly evident from the past, when a plane carrying 151 passengers was hijacked in December 1998, immediately after it took off from Kathmandu Airport. After landing the plane at Kandahar Airport negotiations went on for almost one week for the release of all the passengers safely. Post this hijack, Dilawar Khan would be considered a martyr by the Organisation and would attain a place for himself in Jannat, as assured by the Boss. However, Dilawar Khan knew that he would get the worst of Jahannum if he were to undertake this mission and be responsible for the death of several innocent people.

The second plane was to originate from Afghanistan and would crash into the Bombay Stock Exchange. It was a Kandahar-Mumbai flight. The Boss was in the process of finalising the list of members to undertake this mission. In all probability, this plane would be operated by Bilal, a senior member of the Organisation, who was currently working with a local airline company. No one would suspect anything and also, no weapons would be required in this case. The only thing required was to ensure that Bilal got the duty schedule to fly the plane on that day.

As the days passed by, Dilawar Khan was becoming increasingly nervous about the whole thing. He was not interested in continuing his association with the Organisation in any way and, obviously, did not want to carry out the attacks. Now all he was thinking about was a safe way out of this imbroglio. He had learnt about appreciating the simplicities of life. He was able to understand, appreciate and value the spirituality of this precious life. He deeply respected the positive side of humanity. He wanted to be a part of society anywhere in the world and positively contribute to it as well.

As the day approached, his options were getting limited. Once or twice, he had random thoughts about escaping from the ashram, but he observed that the Boss had woven such an intricate web around the ashram that his every move inside and outside the ashram was being monitored on a real time basis. Any adventurous move by him to escape would have resulted in his immediate capture and severe punishment leading to his death. Consequently, taking a chance to escape was not a very safe option. However, the outcome of this mission would also result in his death in the plane crash. It was a different matter that the death in this case would be glorified by the Organisation as 'Martyrdom' and an act of supreme bravery. He was confused…a death is a death, after all… Did it really matter whether he died while trying to escape from the Organisation or in a suicide attack? While life after death was an uncertainty, the only thing becoming crystal clear and almost certain was that his life in this world was about to end soon. Somehow, he was drawn towards the uncertain certainty rather than the certain uncertainty!

Finally the day arrived. Dilawar Khan woke up early that morning. He was very calm and composed. He finished his early morning prayers and then sat quietly for a while. He needed some time to think about his 'short' future, as it would decide the way he died. But in the end, did it really matter how he died? He did not know. All he knew was that he was going to die. Memorable incidents from his past life, right from his childhood, were flashing in front of his eyes.

And in the spur of a moment, he took a daring decision. He felt that the world should be a better place to live in. He could not contribute much to this cause while he was alive. At least, when he was leaving this world, he wanted to contribute to it positively. Every life saved means the world continued to exist for that person, because as per an old adage, 'It really does not matter whether the world survives or drowns when you die…' He wanted to extend the life of some people at least when he died. There could be small children, women and old people on those planes. They should not have to die because some extremist wants them to, for reasons not connected to them.

He was seeing death in all directions. By default, as per the Boss's plan, he would become a martyr by undertaking his last journey in that flight from Kathmandu to New Delhi. If for some reasons he did not go ahead with this plan, then the Boss would surely kill him. There was no doubt about that. And in very exceptional circumstances, if he managed to escape from the Boss, then the Indian and Pakistani police would track him down sooner or later. So, his chances of living a peaceful life as an ordinary citizen were, at best, very bleak. It was sad how some people made their lives so difficult and complicated by their own choices and actions. No wonder the ancient scriptures laid great emphasis on doing only good deeds always.

As per the plan, Dilawar Khan had left the ashram previous evening and checked into a lodge to avoid any last minute hassles of moving out of the ashram. The Boss had planned to watch the entire episode of the twin bombing live on TV from his rented room outside the ashram. Bilal was to take off from Kandahar as per schedule without appearing suspicious in any manner.

But now, Dilawar Khan had a different plan of action. It was different from all the options available to him at that moment. He thought for one last time and lifted the receiver of the landline phone in his room in the lodge. He dialled a number which he had searched for two days before, ever since this brilliant thought had cropped up in his mind. That number was that of the Inspector General of Prisons, Yashwant Rathore.

Dilawar was calling Yashwant's office phone. He fondly remembered the table and chair in Yashwant's office, where they had spent a good deal of time together during those days when Yashwant had tried to reform Dilawar Khan.

After six rings Yashwant answered the call. He said, 'Good morning, Yashwant Rathore speaking.'

Dilawar Khan said with mixed feelings, 'Yashwant Sahaab, I am Dilawar Khan. Remember me?'

There was silence for a second and then Yashwant said, 'Dilawar Khan? Where are you? How are you?'

Dilawar Khan could sense the kindness in Yashwant's voice. He suddenly got emotional on hearing that familiar, caring voice. He said, 'Sir, I am fine. I am in Nepal now. I have important news to share with you. It is urgent.'

Yashwant was still surprised at this unexpected call from a fugitive criminal. He said, 'Yes Dilawar, go on. Don't think that you can run away for a long time from the law...we will get you soon from wherever you are hiding.'

Dilawar Khan said in a slightly emotional tone, 'Sorry sir, you may not succeed in that. But leave that. If you want to save the lives of around 400 people, please act fast as time is running out. There is going to be a terrorist attack in the next three hours on Mumbai and New Delhi. Two planes are going to crash in India within a gap of fifteen minutes. You can avoid these attacks and save the lives of several innocent people if you take immediate action.'

Yashwant was shocked. He had many questions in his mind. Why was Dilawar Khan informing him about these attacks? How did he know about this? Could these attacks be avoided? Was Dilawar a part of these attacks? He immediately took out his pen and a slip of paper. He said hurriedly, 'Yes Dilawar, go on. I am writing it down.'

'The flight to New Delhi will take off from Kathmandu in the next one hour. But it will not land in New Delhi Airport. It will crash into the Indian Parliament. And the second plane will take off in the next 30 minutes from Kandahar. It is heading to Mumbai. But it will crash into the Bombay Stock Exchange. In the plane from Kathmandu, you will find a terrorist named Parvez who will be in possession of a revolver and some hand grenades. He is a dangerous man. In the plane from Kandahar, the pilot is Bilal. He is a terrorist. He will not be carrying a weapon, as he does not need to. He will 'safely' land the plane on the Bombay Stock Exchange. Apart from several lives being lost, there will be political turmoil and a business shakeout too for a few months because of this...'

Yashwant said, 'Dilawar, are you telling the truth? Why are you telling me all this now? Are you involved in this? Please stop them from doing this...'

Dilawar Khan said in a philosophical tone, 'Sir, please believe me, I am telling the truth. You have limited time to act. Please save India from this disaster. I am telling you this because I owe you something. You were the one who believed in me when I was lodged in the Anda Cell of your jail. You spent hours trying to reform me. Just assume that I am reformed now. Yes, I am also supposed to be involved in this...and I can't stop them from doing this. I would have loved to talk to you for a longer time, but this is an emergency situation and I don't want to come in your way of your exceptional effort at stopping this disaster from happening. Best of luck...'

Yashwant said, 'Dilawar, wait. I am coming to Nepal right away. I shall alert the entire system about this immediately. I want to talk to you. You can still become a good person. I am sure...'

Dilawar Khan interrupted, 'Sir, I have already become a good person. The fact that I am informing you about this plan to attack India itself shows that I am now reformed. The reason I called you was also to talk to you once before I go...'

Yashwant interrupted him and said, 'Dilawar, where are you going? I want to talk to you. Stay there, I am catching the next flight to Kathmandu. Let us meet and talk this over.'

'Sir, you do not get everything you want in life,' said Dilawar. 'I too would have loved to meet you again and get some more lessons on how to become a good person. But it seems like my time is over now. I could not live a life of honour. At least let me have an honourable death. Good bye…may Allah bless you.'

Yashwant heard the phone line go dead on the other side. He had very limited time to act to save the lives of hundreds of innocent people in a terrorist attack, which was supposedly going to happen in the next few hours.

He immediately called the Home Minister, Nandakumar Joshi and explained the emergency to him. Nandakumar in turn alerted the National Investigation Agency and they swung into action. Their first priority was to avoid the planes from taking off, as once the planes took off, the hijackers could dictate terms. Under their control, the planes were like massive petrol bombs floating in the sky, waiting to fall on the desired targets and causing mass destruction of life and property. While Nandakumar and the NIA teams were planning their future action, Yashwant set off for Kathmandu.

The NIA teams quickly divided themselves into two groups to plan their next moves regarding the two planes ready for takeoff: one from Kathmandu and one from Kandahar.

Team A of the NIA called up the Air Traffic Controller of Kathmandu Airport. They wanted to check if the flight had already taken off. The Kathmandu Airport informed them that the flight to New Delhi was already cruising towards the runway for takeoff. The NIA team informed the ATC of Kathmandu about the terrorist's plan and they discussed how they could stop the plane from flying out.

Within few minutes of the discussions, they came up with an idea. The ATC called the pilot of the plane and informed him about the terrorist's plan to crash the plane in India by hijacking it once it took off. They needed to act swiftly without causing any suspicion in Parvez's mind, since he could still cause havoc with the weapons in his possession. They needed to keep the plane parked inside the airport, without allowing anyone to approach the plane. The ATC advised the pilot about their plan. According to the plan, the pilot was going to make an announcement to the passengers that one of the crew members had suffered a heart attack and it was an emergency. A plane's takeoff can be aborted under such emergency situations. In the meantime, the security officers would enter the plane disguised as doctors in white coats with stethoscope hung around their necks. That would give them a suspicion-free access into the plane till they reached Parvez's seat. They had found out by then that Parvez was in Seat 26B, which was an aisle seat. They did not find Dilawar Khan's name. They assumed that he might have used one of his many fake passports. It would be difficult to identify him from among the passengers. But at least they could nab Parvez and then see if they could identify and catch Dilawar Khan as well. To nab Parvez, they just needed to enter the plane dressed as doctors, go near seat 26B and catch him unawares, without giving him the time to react or start any skirmish with his weapons.

The second NIA Team contacted Kandahar Airport and was informed by the ATC that the plane to Mumbai had just taken off. The NIA team quickly explained the situation to them and they discussed how they could control the situation now. The plane was being operated by the terrorist himself and it was nearly impossible to save the lives of passengers and the attack on the BSE. However, after a few minutes of discussions they decided to take a chance. They somehow needed to get in touch with the co-pilot and instruct him to take over the plane. But how were they going to do this? They knew very well that Bilal would not leave the flight controls in the hands of the co-pilot as that would scuttle his plan. Any calls made to the flight by the ATC would be answered by the pilot Bilal himself. They had to do something. The slightest doubt in Bilal's mind would worsen the situation beyond control.

With these thoughts, the ATC team called the plane's cockpit. Bilal answered. The ATC casually asked him about the weather conditions. Bilal answered coolly that the weather conditions were normal. The ATC disconnected. They could not stretch the discussion further without raising suspicion in his mind. But time was running out for them. The plane had already covered one fourth of the distance and would reach Mumbai in a couple of hours.

Meanwhile, on the Kathmandu-New Delhi Flight, the pilot made an announcement to the passengers that one of their crew members had suffered a heart attack and the plane was being taken back to the parking bay for disembarking the patient, who was an air hostess. Parvez turned restless at this announcement as the delay could upset the timing of their attacks. However, he could do nothing about it, other than to wait for the plane to take off after the air hostess was disembarked. As the plane stopped in the parking bay, a ladder was connected to the plane. Immediately, the emergency door of the plane was opened and four doctors entered and started walking through the aisle towards the rear of the plane where the air hostess was supposed to have been lying. The doctors looked carefully all over the plane and particularly at seat 26B. Parvez sat seemingly unperturbed although he was actually worried by these developments, because the plan was to strike the two targets within a gap of 15 minutes.

Now, that calculation would go awry and the gap would be longer. As the doctors hurriedly went past his seat, he noticed something unusual. He heard their footsteps till they went past him and then there was silence. He turned around to see what was happening and in a split second, the two doctors, who were actually heavily built commandoes, pounced on him. They caught him and the other two doctors joined them to keep him under control. There was chaos inside the plane over this unexpected development. Some tense passengers began shouting, getting up from their seats in panic. Immediately, the four commandoes grabbed Parvez and lifted him from his seat. They took him out of the plane and quickly searched and recovered the revolver and some ammunition from his jacket. Simultaneously, two more commandos entered the plane and visually scanned the other passengers to identify any other suspect inside the plane. According to the plan, Dilawar Khan was also supposed to be in the plane. However, they could not find him. The plane was now safe. An announcement was made inside the plane to pacify the anxious passengers and they were told about the terrorist's plan to crash it into the Parliament in New Delhi. All the passengers were relieved at this miraculous escape from a near certain death, had the flight taken off. They were all in a shocked yet joyous mood, congratulating one another on their great escape.

The other NIA Team was in constant touch with the Kandahar ATC. The Kandahar ATC waited for another 10 minutes and took another chance. They called the cockpit and this time the call was answered by the co-pilot, Kamaal. The ATC quickly said, 'Kamaal, this is an emergency. Where is Bilal?'

Kamaal answered, 'He has gone to the toilet. You want to speak to him?'

ATC said, 'No. But listen carefully. Bilal is a terrorist and he plans to crash this aircraft into the Bombay Stock Exchange. Please do something and stop him from doing that. Take the help of some crew members and keep him out of the cockpit. This is a real emergency…'

Suddenly Kamaal interrupted, 'Oh yes, fine. No problem, we shall take care. Bilal is back. Would you like to speak to him? Ok bye…' And he hung up. Kamaal had used his presence of mind to make it appear as though it was a casual conversation, yet signal the ATC that Bilal was back in the cockpit.

The ATC hung up too. They were worried about how Kamaal would handle the situation. They realised that Kamaal had abruptly cut the conversation to prevent Bilal from getting suspicious. They were relieved that at least they had managed to convey the message to Kamaal.

After about five minutes, Kamaal left the cockpit on the pretext of using the toilet. He went to the crew area at the back and spoke to a group of three crew members, two females and one male. He said, 'Guys, there is a problem. I got information from ATC that Bilal is a terrorist and he is planning to crash this plane into the Bombay Stock Exchange. He is not carrying a weapon, but as he is controlling the flight, he can do anything. We need to get him out of the cockpit and keep him out till I land the plane.'

Jane, one of the air hostesses, said, 'Kamaal, but how do we control him outside the cockpit? If he senses that we are trying to keep him forcibly outside the cockpit, he may turn violent and can cause injuries to the passengers or even us…'

Simon, the purser, said, 'Don't worry, once we bring him out of the cockpit, Kamaal can lock the cockpit from inside. That solves half our problem. Then we will physically overpower him by using all our force. He should not be allowed to even move, as he can be extremely dangerous. He is already on a suicide mission, so he will not care for anything anyway.'

Kamaal said, 'Please identify three or four passengers who are strong enough to assist us in this exercise'. Accordingly, Simon made a round of the entire plane walking through the aisle, looking at all the passengers with a smile on his face. He then signalled three of the passengers to follow him to the rear of the plane, where the air hostesses prepare the food trolleys. The three passengers were surprised, as rarely do crew members ask passengers to follow them. Kamaal quickly explained the situation to them and asked for their help. They all agreed.

After a minute's discussion, they made the plan. According to the plan, Kamaal would return to the cockpit soon to avoid any suspicion. After a while, Jane would call the cockpit and seek Bilal's help in sorting out an altercation between two 'irate passengers' fighting over use of toilet. As soon as Bilal came out of the cockpit, Kamaal would lock it from inside. Then, as Bilal came near the rear toilets where the 'physical fight' between two passengers was going on, the third passenger, along with Simon, would pounce on him and hold him, while the two fighting passengers would quickly handcuff him with ropes. That would make them 100% safe. The plan was all set. Any mistake would land all of them in deep trouble. They had to succeed in their efforts. Death was the only other option and it was not desirable to any of them.

All of them wished each other good luck with a raised thumb. They were going to enact the most important drama in their lives. Their efforts were going to save several lives including their own. They needed to get it right.

As planned, Kamaal casually went inside the cockpit and took his seat. He looked out of the front glass window, at the white clouds going past them at great speeds. He appeared very relaxed outwardly, but was extremely tense from within. Glancing at Bilal, he wondered how a person who was on a suicide mission could be so calm.

After about seven minutes, Jane called the cockpit phone. Bilal picked up the receiver and said, 'Hello?'

Jane said, 'Bilal, there is a small issue here. Two passengers are fighting over using the toilet. They are not listening to me. Could you intervene please?'

Bilal did not want any distractions in his goal. He was looking forward to a 'smooth crash' without any disturbance. 'Are they not listening to you?'

Jane replied, 'No Bilal, I tried. All the other passengers are getting disturbed because of them.'

Bilal said, 'Ok, I am coming.' And he turned to Kamaal and signalled that he would be back soon. Kamaal was relieved. He casually signalled 'ok' and kept looking at the dashboard gauges. He had to appear absolutely normal and calm, though a storm was actually brewing inside his mind, to save his and the passenger's lives from this direct threat. Bilal left the cockpit to resolve the issue between the two passengers.

After Bilal left, Kamaal quickly got up and locked the cockpit door without making any sound. After locking it, he just stood for a while, relieved that the plane was safe now. However, he was worried about the next part, which was yet to happen, and unfortunately, he could not take part in that action. He just prayed and hoped for the best.

Bilal walked through the aisle looking towards the rear end toilets, where two passengers were having a heated argument. He also noticed that one more passenger was standing near the toilet waiting for the brawl to get over so that he could use the toilet. He turned around and saw Simon walking behind him. The trap was well set. Bilal approached the passengers and asked them, 'Sir, what is the problem? May I help you?'

One of the passengers said nervously, 'Who are you to interfere? Get lost…'

Bilal said, 'Sir, I am the pilot of this plane. I shall do my best to…'

As he spoke, suddenly Simon caught him from behind and the two fighting passengers along with the passenger waiting to use the toilet bent over him, holding him tight on the floor. As expected, there was panic among the passengers and some of them got up from their seats not knowing what was happening. The four men quickly took Bilal to a rear seat in the plane and tied him to the seat and stood guarding him. Bilal realised, that somehow these people had come to know about his plan but kept quiet without resisting. He was thinking about the Boss's reaction at the failure of his plan.

The Boss was watching TV in anticipation, waiting for the big news to be flashed across all the news channels about the twin terrorist attacks in India. However, as the expected time of crash passed by, there was no news at all. He began to get worried. He asked one of his boys to find out whether the flight to New Delhi had taken off from Kathmandu Airport. And he came to know that the flight had been delayed by one hour due to some 'technical snag' but the flight had now taken off and was on the way. Similarly, he also enquired from Kandahar Airport and came to know that the flight to Mumbai had taken off as per schedule and was expected to land in Mumbai soon. He was happy. The only snag was that the timing between the two crashes would be different now. He had planned the New Delhi strike first and the Mumbai strike fifteen minutes later. But now, the schedule had changed with a time gap of 45 minutes.

As time passed by, both the flights landed without any incident. The Boss was furious when he realised that his grandiose plans of causing havoc and destruction in the political and commercial capitals of India had gone awry. There was no news at all. He tried calling Dilawar Khan, Parvez and Bilal but no one responded to his calls.

As the news broke out in the media that terrorists had planned to crash these two planes, and that the attempt had been foiled by the well coordinated planning between the NIA teams, the ATC teams in Kathmandu and Kandahar and the airport security departments at these two airports, there were scenes of jubilations at Delhi and Mumbai. The passengers and their relatives and friends who had come to receive them started hugging each another and celebrating life. Some emotional people started crying as well, not able to contain their happiness. Such attempts by the terrorists are done after a lot of study, proper homework and a systematic plan. They rarely fail. However, in this case, these people were the lucky ones who had survived. They were destined to live longer.

Meanwhile, one NIA team had reached Kathmandu. Initially Yashwant had wanted to join them, but then at the last minute, he dropped the idea. He felt his primary responsibility was managing the prison, not catching the criminals. That was the job of another team. He respected the responsibilities of each department and on ethical grounds, did not want to interfere in their functioning.

The NIA team raided the lodge from where the phone call was made to Yashwant. The room, from where the call had been made, was closed from inside. The NIA team with the support of the local police broke open the door and...found Dilawar Khan lying in a pool of blood. He was holding a revolver with a silencer in his right hand. He had shot himself in the forehead.

The team was shocked to see this gruesome sight. While it appeared to be a case of suicide, they needed to be sure. An investigation team does not arrive at any conclusion till it is able to gather evidence from the scene of crime supported by a clear motive behind the crime. They did not rule out the possibility of it being a murder till there were sufficient evidences to suggest otherwise. They quickly looked around to see whether there were any leads or evidence which could help them to logically arrive at a conclusion. The room did not show any signs of a scuffle or fight. While they were looking around, one of them noticed an envelope on the table. The envelope was addressed to Yashwant Rathore and was classified as 'Important' on the top left corner. It was a sealed envelope. The investigating team collected the envelope as a crucial piece of evidence but decided not to open it on ethical grounds. The photographers took pictures of the body from all angles possible for further investigation.

By evening that day, the Breaking News flashing on all the news channels was about how the possible terrorist attack on the two most important places in India had been foiled by the quick and coordinated actions of the various security agencies involved. The country was in a state of shock. However, everyone was happy that the attack had been thwarted by the quick action of Yashwant Rathore who alerted the Home Ministry who in turn took the necessary actions just in time to save the lives of so many people. The Boss was terribly upset at this sudden turn of events and was still unclear about who had leaked the news to the security agencies and at what stage. That morning, everything had seemed to be going as per plan. He was also worried on hearing that Dilawar Khan had died in what seemed to be a suicide attempt while Bilal and Parvez were in the custody of the investigating agencies. He wondered whether Dilawar Khan had leaked the information to the Indian authorities before he killed himself. But then, there was no reason for him to do so, as Dilawar Khan was a trusted man of the Organisation. While the Boss knew that Dilawar had strayed from his path for a while, it was unthinkable that he could have done something like this to the Organisation.

The NIA team returned to India and met Yashwant to hand over the envelope; they were also curious to know what was in this letter written by a terrorist just before committing suicide, to a jailor who had tried to reform him earlier.

Yashwant had mixed feelings when he opened the letter. For some reason, he felt guilty that he had not done enough to save Dilawar Khan's life. He also felt that the last phone call between them a few hours ago had been an emotional one. He wondered whether any other actions could have yielded better results.

With slightly shaky hands, he opened the letter. It appeared to be a lengthy letter. He started reading it…

Dear Yashwant Sahaab,

Assalam aley kum. How are you? It was nice talking to you today. I have a lot to say to you, but unfortunately do not have much time to say it. Most probably, by the time you read this letter, I might already be dead.

Yashwant Sahaab, I was in your jail for just a few months. But those days proved to be a turning point in my life. My outlook towards life changed after your efforts to reform me. Initially I used to mock you and feel pity for your listless pursuit of trying to improve the prisoners' lives. And let me confess to you as well, I was not fully reformed by the time I had escaped from your jail. If I had been reformed fully in the jail, I would not have escaped at all.

After I left your jail, I made one unsuccessful attempt at killing the builder Kripesh Mehta. Whether he was lucky or I did not do my homework well, or it was the first link of a series of coincidences...but I missed shooting him from a point blank range. I immediately fled thereafter to Islamabad.

I was given the assignment of kidnapping the Home Minister Khwaja Salahudeen's daughter for a ransom. Surprisingly, she continued the exercise of reforming me, from where you had left. I would see your reflection in her at times when she preached morality to me. Those 36 hours spent with her consolidated the values you had sown in my sub-conscious mind. She almost changed my life and my way of thinking. I admired her knowledge at such a young age. Of course, a large part of the credit goes to her parents as well, for instilling such good values in her. The purity of her thoughts was strong enough to shake my beliefs and faith in terrorism. She made me realise that there is a good world outside, a world which I had not experienced. That was when I defied my Boss and the Organisation for the first time, and escaped from the scene without harming her, by disobeying his instructions.

I needed to be away from the Organisation for some time to take important decisions about the way I was going to spend the rest of my life. I was almost reformed. I had to take care not to be traced by them otherwise they would drag me into the same arena again. There was no exit from our world leading to some safe and secure place on this earth. One could only die to be away from the Organisation. And I wanted to live... desperately.

I escaped to Nepal and took shelter in an ashram. I was thrilled to work there disguised as a gardener. Over a period of a few months, I planted several trees in that ashram. I felt so happy to see these trees grow leaf by leaf every day. A new flower on any one of them would give me immense pleasure. I was actually feeling as though I was giving a life to something which lives. That feeling was extremely satisfying and gave me absolute contentment. I am happy that even after I am gone, the trees planted by me will continue to grow new leaves and flowers for many more years to come.

In the ashram, I heard several discourses by many religious saints and I was completely reformed. With each lecture I attended, I was gaining divine messages contained in ancient Hindu wisdom. Unfortunately, today the wisdom is available in abundance on the Internet but there are very few takers. Earlier, people had to go in search of ancient scriptures, which were only available in the form of old fragile books in the possession of a few learned people who could share their knowledge. Today, there is the omniscient Internet which has all the knowledge in the world. It humbles a human to know that the knowledge contained on the Internet is far more than what a large group of intellectuals can store in their minds. But sadly, people have displaced their priorities today.

When something is available in abundance, its value is lost quickly. The same is happening with the knowledge available on the Internet. Instead of valuing it, they take it for granted. Human life is short. It is less than one hundred years. One cannot grasp the entire knowledge contained in the Universe in one life. Therefore, one needs to prioritise what he needs to learn. Unfortunately, people today try to learn only that which can fetch them money. They are after money, not values. But unfortunately, they all forget that true happiness comes from values and not from money. If it were not so, the richest people in this world would have also been the happiest people in this world.

I was getting enlightened with each of religious discourse and decided to never ever go back to the Organisation. And that is when Destiny had something else in its mind. Somehow I was traced by the Organisation and the Boss appeared in front of me, from out of the blue, one day. He needed me because they had trained me. I was good at what I did for them. They did not want to let me go so easily. And he persuaded me by force to execute this one last assignment of the plane crash. I realised, that if I disobeyed him, he would instantly kill me. So, I had to act as though I was 'reformed' after being 'swayed' temporarily from the original 'good path' as understood by the Organisation. But my mind was rebelling against the plan. I needed to escape from this situation. And there was no way in sight to do so.

That is when I decided to take this extreme step. After all, even if I am reformed, I had to pay for the sins I had committed in the past. My reformation does not have the powers to wash away those sins. I realised the pain which I had inflicted on so many people in the various attacks I carried out around the world. Some people were dead while many others were permanently injured in those attacks. Some had a disabled person to look after for life. I had to repay this debt to the Almighty. No one who commits a crime can go scot free ever. It is foolish to assume that by fooling the Governments, we can live unpunished. There is one Government which sits at the top and no one can fool that. It watches everyone, at every moment. While many have to repay for the sins committed by them here on this Earth in this life itself, some carry it forward in their next Janma, as a negative opening balance in accounting parlance.

Dear Yashwant Sahaab, I think I have bored you enough. I take your leave now. I hope you were able to avoid the twin terrorist attacks in Mumbai and New Delhi. I did not want to get caught either by the Organisation or the police of any country. Everyone is not as kind as you, who nurtures a fond hope and dream of reforming criminals.

Please continue to be the way you are…always be positive and optimistic. The world surely needs more and more people like you. Hindus believe that people are born again in this world through reincarnation. I hope to take birth again and see a better world. And if I happen to see one, then I can vouch that it was because of people like you and your relentless efforts.

Please forgive me for any mistakes committed by me… I know I did many grave ones. But then, all sins committed in ignorance can be expiated. I too hope to be clear of my guilty conscious one day.

Take good care of yourselves and the world... Khuda Hafiz...!

Yours,

Dilawar Khan.

Yashwant was silent for a while after reading the letter. Without his knowledge, tears were rolling down his eyes. He did not know whether these were tears of sadness due to the loss of a person known to him, or of happiness to see a person reformed by his efforts, or simply the emotions of a common man.

For the past few months, he had been praying and 'Ordering' his sub-conscious mind that Dilawar Khan should be reformed. He had been so anxious to see the results of his efforts all these days. He'd persistently continued with his mission all along, but now, when he came to know that he had actually been successful in achieving his goal, he was sad. The theory of the sub-conscious mind had really worked perfectly well for him. It had literally transformed a hardcore terrorist into a God-fearing person with noble thoughts. Ironically, it felt like: 'Operation Successful but Patient Dead'.

He handed over the letter to the investigating agencies for their further investigations and sat in his office chair for a long time. He had no enthusiasm to even get up from his chair. He just stared at the second hand on the wall clock, which kept ticking relentlessly at the same speed. He wondered at the mysterious concept of Time. Did people know about Time before watches and clocks were invented? Why is Time so emotionless? Why can't it stop for a while at important times? And then, in the spur of the moment, he made an analogy comparing Time to a cassette player.

A person's lifetime is like a cassette which runs only on 'Play' mode. There is no 'Rewind' or 'Fast Forward' button. One cannot 'Fast Forward' Time, like one would desperately wish during the difficult moments in life. Similarly, there was no 'Rewind' button which meant: one cannot 'relive' the enjoyable moments in the past again. They are gone…forever. There is no 'Slow Motion' either. Time actually keeps running at a constant speed, but a person feels that it is moving very slow in difficult moments, and very fast during enjoyable moments. Finally, there is not even an 'Eject' button. There is only one button - 'Stop' - which is used by the Almighty… only once. Therefore, this world can be compared to one big cassette player with millions of slots for cassettes. The Almighty just keeps inserting cassettes and takes them out once they have played fully. Some cassettes play longer than others.

So mysterious…this concept of Time!

Chapter 16

Dilawar Khan's letter was released by the NIA to the Home Ministry who promptly released it to the media. And by evening, the contents of the letter were available on every news channel and news websites. Everyone was surprised to know the events mentioned in the letter. Rarely in history had a terrorist detailed out his honest thoughts like this in an open letter. The letter was a testimony that Yashwant's efforts had not gone in vain. Yashwant almost became a hero overnight. He started getting invitations from various news channels to appear on their TV shows to discuss his efforts in reforming all the prisoners in general and Dilawar Khan in particular.

Yashwant was happy on one account: his theory of using the power of the sub-conscious mind for bringing about a positive change in someone had worked. He had consistently and relentlessly wished, visualised and felt that Dilawar Khan had reformed. And against all odds, Dilawar Khan had indeed been reformed. It was another matter that he did not get an opportunity to live his life as a reformed person long enough. Destiny finally catches up with every one and one has to settle his 'current account' of deeds before departing from Earth. What happens thereafter is only a theory and not substantiated as yet. Different religions say different things about what happens after death. Some believe in re-birth of the soul in a different body, while some say that the dead body does experience feelings of pain and pleasure inside the grave for a long time after he/she has died. No one in history has so far come back from wherever, to inform others about his experiences after death.

Yashwant started analysing all the events mentioned in Dilawar Khan's letter. He was now wondering whether the powers of sub-conscious mind had really had such a great impact on Dilawar Khan's mind and his thinking. He had experienced the power on smaller matters earlier, but this was the greatest of all experiments conducted yet on the power of the sub-conscious mind by anybody in this world. He was highly enthusiastic and eager to share it with others now. He wanted the world to know about this theory and utilise the tremendous powers hidden in the sub-conscious mind for bringing about positive changes in one's life. The world could become a much better place to live in if even a fraction of the total population experimented with this concept. And soon, he started looking for an opportunity to articulate this to the world. He had already talked about this concept in the interviews given to various media channels but now he felt a forum was necessary so he could address a large gathering of influential people about this.

And he started 'Visualising' the scene. He visualised that *he was giving a spirited speech on the powers of the sub-conscious mind to an international audience in a large auditorium and that the people responded very positively after the speech was over.*

After about a week, he got the opportunity. A conference was scheduled in Mumbai where foreign delegates from all over the world were invited for a 'World Peace Convention'. These delegates were senior officials working in Government and Non-Government Organisations, who could influence the decisions of their respective Governments. And as one of the invitees to address the gathering, Yashwant's name was nominated by the Government of India in consultation with the Government of Maharashtra. This was the opportunity which Yashwant had been desperately waiting for. He needed to wake the world up from its slumber of ignorance and pessimism.

He immediately started preparing a speech for this event. He made several corrections to the draft. Every time he read it, he found some small corrections to be made. Finally, after some 45 version of the original draft, his final speech was ready. It was an opportunity he did not want to miss. He felt that it was his moral duty to enlighten the world about the magical powers of the sub-conscious mind. If people took it seriously, then it had the potential to change the world positively. It was a novel and unique experiment done by an individual to stimulate the thoughts of large sections of people around the world to think positively. The benefits would accrue to future generations apart from helping the present ones immensely.

And finally the day arrived. The function was being telecast live and was held in a large auditorium with a seating capacity of about 10,000 people. They had modern technological audio visual gadgets for the benefit of the large audience watching it live inside the hall and those watching it live on televisions across the world.

The function began at 10.00am as per schedule. Yashwant's speech was at 3.00pm. The word had got around among the participants that Yashwant had worked very hard on his speech for the day. It was also being speculated that he would stress on his now-famous theory of the power of the sub-conscious mind. Most people were excited about the concept, as they had no reason to either strongly believe or disbelieve the theory. Not many people had really experimented with it to have an opinion on it. And since those who had experienced it were very few in numbers, it had not had a great impact on the masses. During lunchtime, the conversations gathered steam and created curiosity about Yashwant's speech. Even world television channels started scrolling the news at the bottom of the screen mentioning Yashwant's much-anticipated speech at the convention.

As the clock struck 3.00pm, everyone was looking forward to this much-awaited programme. When Yashwant was invited onto stage, there was a huge round of applause when he rose to his feet and walked towards the stage. Yashwant had carried his speech with him, because he did not want to miss any of the important points.

He adjusted the mike and looked at the audience. They were waiting with bated breath to listen to him. Yashwant started his historical speech...

'Ladies and Gentlemen, a very good afternoon to all of you. It gives me great pleasure to be amidst you today in this programme on 'World Peace'.

Today the world is passing through a very critical phase. On one hand, there is tremendous development taking place through the application of innovative technology and on the other, there are social disturbances being witnessed in various parts of the world. On one side people are progressing rapidly, while others are being denied even their basic rights to live. A disturbing trend which is being observed across many developing countries is that the rich are getting richer and the poor are getting poorer.

Friends, I have one question to ask. I don't want you to give me an answer right now, but just ask yourself: is this the right kind of development? Is this the correct growth pattern? The way this world is moving, would it make more people happy, or unhappy in due course of time? Who needs to correct the situation? Is someone going to come from space and help us in realising our goals of 'World Peace'? No one is going to come from anywhere. It is up to all of us to sit, think and come out with an action plan on how we want this world to be. And therefore, it is imperative for each one of us to know that we do play a role in this world. We are a part of it. All the great positive and negative deeds in this world are done by someone among us. Each one of us has the potential to make our surroundings either better or worse than before. We have the capacity, capability and the potential. The only problem is that we do not use it as frequently and in the required measure.

Friends, do not lead your life as though you are a guest on this Earth, who has come here for a few years and will go away when your time is up. It is your responsibility to ensure that you pass on this Earth to the future generations in the same or better condition. You have no right to damage it or spoil it in any manner whatsoever. When we borrow something from our neighbour, we return it in same condition, right? The same logic applies here as well. We have received this Earth from our ancestors. We need to hand it over in a better condition to our future generations.

Sadly, we are not doing that right now. We have become too selfish, always thinking about our own interests. Forget the future generations; we fight amongst ourselves for the limited resources available today. The Gulf countries have been subjected to innumerable hostilities ever since oil deposits were discovered there a few decades back. It makes me shudder to imagine that the coming decades are going to witness full scale wars being fought over water deposits. The same water which our forefathers took for granted as a free natural resource is no longer a free resource. Who would have thought fifty years back that people would be buying water in bottles while travelling? And what guarantee do we have today that we may not have to purchase clean air fifty years from now?

Thanks to the rapidity with which we are spoiling this beautiful environment, we are surely inviting a calamity sooner or later. Why does no developed nation want to curtail it's contribution of carbon emissions when scientists world over are crying themselves hoarse saying that excessive carbon emission is the foremost reason for the increased incidence of floods and tsunamis across the world? Just because it does not affect them directly, is it fair on their part to continue to wreck the planet's eco-system? How can a sane country forget that we all share the same Earth after all? There is no alternative invented as of now for rehabilitating mankind in case of a big threat to Earth's longevity. We all are destined to live on this Earth and die on this Earth only. Then why does this simple wisdom elude their collective intelligence?

Friends, I am also equally worried about the way we behave as an international community. Why is it that some nations try to exercise their powers over other nations that are weaker than them? Does it ever happen in a good cultured family that a stronger brother bullies the weaker brother? Are we not brothers living in one big family in this world? Who has given any one of us the right to interfere with and intimidate others for malicious reasons? If we are to progress, we progress together only and not in bits and pieces. Unfortunately, over the last few centuries, the mightier countries have started taking the law into their hands, disobeying the law set up by international confederations and global bodies. Such acts will only provide fodder to negativity in deprived countries and create a situation where anti-social elements flourish. These elements ask one simple question: why are they living in penury when so many others are living in luxury? Unfortunately, history shows that one country with such negative thoughts can create panic in all its neighbouring countries about their safety. And when we have many such negative countries, they form a nexus to fight it out together. Finally, all of us will be the losers. How can anyone claim victory when it is built over the destruction of someone else? In the epic story of the 'Mahabharata', the Pandavas say at one point during the war, 'What is the use of our victory when it is achieved by annihilating our own brothers?' The sanctity of any victory is lost when unfair means are adopted and unjust force is used against the well-laid principles of humanity.

It is in this context that I want to draw your attention to the fact that you can make a change. Yes, YOU can make a change. Every single person can contribute in rolling the juggernaut of positive change around the world. You might say, 'I am too small to bring about any change in this vast system.' But then if you think like this, let me tell you, you are sadly mistaken. Each one of us is endowed with an exceptionally powerful gift by Nature, which very few people know how to use. Many of us are even oblivious to this gift. Yes, I am talking about the secret and mysterious power of the sub-conscious mind. Our sub-conscious mind is one of the most powerful tools anyone can possess. And yet, many of us do not even know about its existence. The sub-conscious mind of every person is connected with one another through a central server. That central server is what we refer to as the Almighty, Nature, God, Fate and Destiny. All of us believe that Nature's powers are limitless, right? Who can withstand the fury of a hurricane or a tornado or a tsunami or an earthquake? Human beings are too weak to resist and challenge Nature's powers. Imagine, if you gain access to this power, how would it be? Unbelievable, right? But it is true.

Every person can use his sub-conscious mind's powers to make the desired incidents happen as per his wishes. The sub-conscious mind is almost thirty thousand times more powerful than our conscious mind. The trick is very simple. Have faith and belief in something which you want to happen and your sub-conscious mind will automatically transmit these waves through the central server to other sub-conscious minds which will start acting in such a way that your faith and belief becomes a reality. It does not cost a penny. It does not require a rigorous physical workout for extended periods. What it requires is only that you start visualising the desired outcome in front of your eyes. You do it regularly and you are bound to experience a change around you in just a few days, sometimes in a few weeks.

There are several books written on this subject by eminent authors who have done in-depth studies on this subject and practiced it successfully. They have even narrated their personal experiences on how they have achieved even seemingly impossible looking tasks easily by practicing this method.

I have only one appeal. I request you to please use this method for the betterment of this world. Let this world be a better place to live in. Let our future generations not live in a state of deficiency, uncertainty and acrimony. Let there be abundance everywhere and let people be happy. Let adults learn to live in as joyous a state as the children. Let everyone have a trust in all others. Let no country suspect its neighbours of possessing wrong intentions or indulging in nefarious activities clandestinely. Let the birds continue to chirp at dawn and dusk. Let animals live free of any danger of being poached by the human race. Let the flowers bloom in abundance and enliven the atmosphere. Let the trees give us juicy fruits and spread their branches far and wide to provide us shade in our hours of need. Let us all respect each other. Let people speak to one another openly and freely without any ulterior motives or intentions. Let people start respecting one another's religions and faiths. Let the fish in aquariums be as happy as those swimming in the vast open seas. Let children be taught good values at the right time so they realise what is good and bad for them. Let them develop an ability to judge a righteous path from a path of dishonour and ignominy.

I sincerely request you, urge you and plead with you to please give a serious thought to my words. Please use the powers of your sub-conscious mind for not just your personal benefit but also for the benefit of your family, your community, your city, your country and this beautiful world. Remember that we are highly blessed to be here right now, alive and thinking. We may not be there tomorrow. Can anyone guarantee that he will be alive tomorrow? I would laugh at that person's immaturity in not realizing that the only uncertain thing in this world is life. While each one of us knows very well that we shall be leaving this world one day, without taking anything with us, no one actually thinks about his death. We conveniently assume that it is way too far for us, to bother about it right now. But you never know. The only thing you are sure about is the present moment. You have the legitimate right to only the breath inside your lungs as of now. Even the next breath is not guaranteed.

So, please use your 'Present' for a constructive purpose. Please make a change to someone around you. Please contribute to building your nation. If I could change the life of a hardcore terrorist with my sustained efforts, one who had been thoroughly brainwashed by the Organisation, you can do that too. Let me reveal some of the secrets about my trials and experiments in using these powers on the most difficult cause... that of reforming the terrorist called Dilawar Khan.

At first, I thought that it was highly improbable and rather insane to even hope for any such change to happen through these powers. But then, as I practiced it successfully day after day, I could sense that I was on the right track. Now, when I look back at all the events after his audacious escape from my jail, I can distinctly see that at every step, there has been an influence of the natural force. I alone could not have made it happen.

I cite my first indication of the powers working for me, when, on the day of escape, Shakeel was left behind. As per the plan, both Dilawar Khan and Shakeel were supposed to escape. However, at the last minute, Shakeel slipped for apparently no reason, while running to catch the helicopter. And Dilawar Khan was forced to leave him behind. Shakeel's survival was very important for us because, from him, we got leads that the Organisation had planned to kill a builder from South Mumbai. We immediately started doing research and identified Kripesh

Mehta as the most likely target. We had enough time to provide him with protection and make necessary security arrangements for him. That saved his life eventually. So, there was a purpose for Shakeel to slip and be left behind...the purpose was to save the Kripesh's life.

The next assignment Dilawar Khan had was to kidnap Maliha, the daughter of Pakistan's Home Minister, Khwaja Salahudeen. Here too, my powers worked. To implement his plan, Dilawar Khan had joined Maliha's school as a Physical Instructor. During the days he worked in the school, he came close to seeing the innocence in this world on the faces of young children. The tender human being inside the terrorist Dilawar Khan had woken up. He started seeing the world from a different perspective altogether. He realised for the first time that the world is a very happy place to live, seeing the smiles on children's faces.

He kidnapped Maliha and that is where Nature's powers assisted me in my goal. Apparently, Maliha discussed so much religion, politics, good values etc with him that he was forced to reconsider his original mission. He was partially reformed during those 36 hours. He realised that there was someone who was more interested in developing Pakistan than caring for his daughter's life. He was exposed for the first time to such rare qualities of honesty and devotion to the country. He realised that he should not be an impediment to Pakistan's development. However, he was chained to the ideology of the Organisation and was bound to obey their instructions blindly, without asking any questions.

Therefore, he chose to escape from the guest house without harming Maliha. He had decided to defy the orders of his Organisation for the first time since he had joined them. Once he escaped from the scene, he felt light, as if tons of burdens were removed from his shoulders. He wanted to live a life like a free bird, without any worry about the people from the

Organisation or the police catching up with him. For that, he needed to become incognito for some time and he chose to go to Nepal so that he could be away from the glare for some time.

In Kathmandu, the fact that he chose to work in an ashram shows the directive from natural forces again because that is where his reformation was complete. He happened to listen to several discourses there. He loved to water the trees and used to feel untold joy to see a new flower born on a small sapling. He spent some of the happiest days of his life in the ashram.

However, his happiness was short lived, as he was soon spotted by the Organisation's men and they came there to recapture him and brainwash him for the next assignment. He had to act as though he was reformed, only to gain some time to think. Otherwise they would have got him killed without the slightest hesitation.

After much thought, he decided to die honourably, at least saving a few lives in the process. A life saved by him cannot justify or compensate for a life taken by him earlier, but at least the intensity and magnitude of his sins in his conscience would have reduced. So, he called me to save the lives of a few hundred people and the rest is history. I consider it my personal victory that I was able to reform him remotely, while I had absolutely no control over him in whatsoever manner. Nature's forces sided with me in my ambition of reforming Dilawar Khan. Nature's forces brought forward certain situations in his life which reformed him eventually. However, the fact that he died in the process only goes to show that every criminal has to pay for his deeds at one time or another. And Dilawar Khan too paid a price for his inglorious past.

In fact, I now feel that the reason for his escape from my prison was towards the fulfilment of my belief in world peace and ensuring that innocent people are saved. If Dilawar Khan had not escaped then, the Organisation would have probably assigned some other terrorist for this mission and today we would have had a national disaster due to this twin attack. Many times, some things happen in our lives which we have no clue about. We do not realise their importance till much later, when things begin to unfold at an appropriate time. However, we are too small to understand the cause for such happenings. At the same time, it sometimes appears that it is a blessing that we do not know the reasons for every incident happening in our lives. If we were to know our future in advance, feelings like excitement, suspense, thrill, happiness, joy etc would not be experienced by anyone. In such a scenario, everything would be known, and our lives would become almost like stereotyped movie shooting sequences where everyone knows what is going to happen to him in due course of time.

Friends, I stop here. I hope to have sufficiently ignited your minds about the theory of the sub-conscious mind. Please use it for the betterment of this world. Let the world remember you as a contributor and not a spectator to what happened here, while you were here. Remember, none of those who are alive today will be around after 100 years. Yet, the world will continue to survive and grow. The world will be full of new people. Please act today in a way that will attract an applause and admiration from those who will inherit this Earth decades and centuries after we have gone.

All of us have heard that there is tremendous strength in unity. Please use your unity for the noble cause of global peace and harmony. Make a strong global union for this cause cutting across religion and nationalities. Usually, trade unions are looked at with respect by labourers and with disdain by managements all over the world. But in this case, I assure you, if you make a union of people wishing good about humanity and mankind, the ultimate manager of this world is going to be humbled and overawed at your demands. He would love you immensely. He would bow in front of you with affection, as he always loves to see his creations in a happy and peaceful state. He created this world for all of us to enjoy each and every moment. He created this world so that we can understand his true powers, his very existence in an invisible form everywhere around us and to revere him. Every religion lays great emphasis on worshipping the Lord and in believing in his powers. Let us make him happy by our collective action of trying to bring peace and prosperity to his creation. His creation is the sole basis of our existence. Without it, we are nowhere.

So, please leave your imprint on this planet. Use your hidden potential to help those around you. Make a positive difference in someone else's life. It is very satisfying experience. Even animals live for themselves. But those who live for others are the real heroes in this world. We need to emulate them and draw inspiration from them. You do not need someone to invite you to start doing good work for society. It is your Inner Self which should push you into doing that. And there is no specific or auspicious time to start this initiative. You can start from tomorrow, or today, or even this moment.

Be a changed personality from now on. Search for opportunities to help others. Use your hidden powers to uplift the deprived sections of society. God loves such people. I hope and wish that you all practice this technique of awakening the power of your sub-conscious mind; it will help the world in general. If I could reform a hardcore terrorist using this technique, imagine what you all can do collectively if you decide. You can undoubtedly make this world a much better place for everyone to live in.

With these words, I conclude my speech. May God bless you all…'

As Yashwant concluded his address, there was a thunderous applause for almost five minutes. It was as though everyone in the auditorium was momentarily transported into another world, an imaginary world which was full of optimism and positivity. They all came out of the trance once the speech was over. The millions of people watching the address live on the television were also glued till the last word. It was as if the world had stopped its business and listened carefully to this spirited speech from a person who had successfully used the infinite power of his sub-conscious mind for a very noble purpose. He had saved several precious lives by persistently trying to reform Dilawar Khan, and finally reforming him. It was another matter that Dilawar Khan had chosen not to live in his reformed state. Probably his reformed mind had been too guilty about his past and had not allowed him to live in peace with himself.

From the next day onwards, there was a marked increase in the number of people attending camps organised by Yogeshwar and other enlightened people who had successfully used this technique in various countries. Bookshops witnessed a sharp increase in the sale of books on the subject. Search engines saw a huge jump in the number of people visiting websites giving any information on the subject.

There was a gradual awakening in people all over the world. People realised that they had the power to change their own and other's fate to a certain extent at least, if not fully. And the word spread quickly that it works. People were inspired by the video of the speech on YouTube.

A sense of goodness was prevailing in society. People were now more eager to help others in need. They started listening to others with attention and care. Orphanages and old age homes across the globe started receiving large amounts in donations. People began to feel that they were in fact a part of a large global family. There was no malice in anyone's behaviour. Everyone talked of peace, happiness and overall growth for everyone.

One year later

Yashwant woke up from sleep one Sunday morning and went straight to his favourite armchair in the lawns of his house. The day's newspapers were already placed there. He casually glanced through them and was surprised to see the positive headlines. The terrorism cells across the world were either getting closed down or the members were being captured. Terrorists were becoming extinct like dinosaurs. It was such a pleasing thought.

The other headline said that the talks between Arab countries and Israel were progressing on a highly positive note with several bilateral and multilateral pacts signed for mutual trade and investment benefits. Just below that, there was a news item which described the merger of South Korea and North Korea, just like East and West Germany had merged a few years ago.

He flipped the main page and saw another news item about India and Pakistan resolving the age old Kashmir issue amicably, with both parties excited at the solution. The people of the Kashmir region were the biggest beneficiaries of the solution, as they had suffered for several decades on this very issue with both sides staking claim for their ownership.

In the business section of the newspaper, there was very interesting news about the establishment of a global charity foundation for helping needy people all over the world. This trust received contributions and donations from wealthy individuals from all over the world and the office bearers were drawn from all countries, big and small. So, every decision was whetted by every country. The decisions were largely pertaining to sending the aid for victims of earthquakes, famines, floods, tsunamis, typhoons and hurricanes. These natural calamities did not know national boundaries and could strike anytime anywhere. All countries were equally vulnerable for one kind of a threat or the other.

The spiritual section of the newspaper carried positive quotes from all religions. These quotes reminded readers about their purpose on Earth and how to lead peaceful and happy lives.

The international section of the newspaper referred to a confidential report which suggested that the terrorist camps all over the world were closing down dramatically in the recent past. The main reasons cited for this abrupt closure were lack of funds, shortage of new recruits and an increased crackdown by the law enforcement agencies around the world.

Yashwant was surprised. All this was happening so soon… In fact he had 'Visualised' all of these things and 'Believed' that one day they would become a reality. However, he was not sure whether the collective power of the people around the world had helped to accelerate it at such a fast pace. He smiled satisfactorily...his mission was now fulfilled.

And then, while placing his cup on the centre table, it fell down. He quickly bent forward to pick it up…and woke up from his sleep. So, he was dreaming about all this…?

Wow…what a wonderful dream it was. He was so happy to have dreamt about such a positive world. He believed that one day this would be a reality.

It was Sunday morning. So, he went to his favourite lawn chair to read the newspapers. He opened the newspaper…

Would he find the news which he had read about in his dreams?

Would he ever read such news in the newspapers?

Would the collective power of sub-conscious minds of millions of people in this world have the power to change global destiny?

Above all, is destiny changeable?

If it is so, how can it be called Destiny?

Maybe it will still be called Destiny…

Altered Destiny.

Books by same author

Power Games of Life

Today we find that many people are blindly running after their careers, positions of power and accumulation of material wealth. But all of this is not guaranteed to give a person peace of mind, which is the most essential requirement for a contented life.

'Power Games of Life' is a fast paced book which touches upon the changes in ideologies of four childhood friends over five decades of their lives. It talks about the compromises some people have to make to reach their goals in life.

Reaching the 'destination of life' is least important. The way we reach that point defines 'how' we have lived our life. And it may come as a surprise to many, that often a simple lifestyle can bring a person immense satisfaction and joy.

The book is a unique blend of motivation, philosophy and pragmatism about life. The reader is left to judge which of the four friends was happiest in his sixties.